WHAT THE DOCTOR ORDERS

A SINGLE DADDY DOCTOR ROMANCE (SAVED BY THE DOCTOR BOOK TWO)

MICHELLE LOVE

IVY WONDER

CONTENTS

BLURB

I wasn't looking for love when it found me in my backyard...
My neighbor's son came in and stole my heart, then his father did the same.
Nothing had ever been easier than being with him.
His gaze set me ablaze, his soft whispers turned me into a puddle of lust, and his touch blew me away.
As easy as it was to be with him, to let him into my heart, and to fall deeply in love—I knew his son came first. And I agreed—at the time.
But love doesn't let us wait sometimes—and this was one of those times.
I didn't have only one person to convince not to throw our love away, I had three.
A daunting task to say the least, but one well worth taking on. For a love like ours only comes around once in a lifetime and that makes it well worth fighting for...

1

HARMAN

"Morning, Skye. How're you feeling?"

Seeing a sick or injured child's eyes open after surgery always fills me with something that nothing else can. There are definitely some perks to being a pediatric surgeon.

His mother and father flanked me on either side as I checked in on their son after removing a bullet that had lodged near his spinal cord. Both doctors themselves, they knew how dangerous the surgery had been.

Doctor Dawson, the boy's father, moved forward, running his hand over his look-alike son's dark brow. "I know it hurts to talk. Nod if you're feeling okay."

The boy's head moved a tiny bit—definitely better than nothing. "Good. You might not feel great right now, but you'll feel better every day, Skye." I turned to face his mother next. Having a son myself, I knew how hard this had to be for them. "He's going to be okay, Doctor Storey. The operation wasn't difficult. The hardest part now will be the recovery, both physical and emotional, after the horrible ordeal you've all been through."

Doctor Storey's auburn curls bounced around her shoulders as she nodded. "I've already got a therapist lined up. She'll be seeing

Skye as soon as he can talk. I don't want this to damage him any deeper than it has to."

As I placed my hand on her shoulder, I felt my cell buzzing in my pocket. "I'll leave you guys alone. I'll come back later to check on him."

"Thanks, Doctor Hunter." The poor child's mother went to stand on the other side of her son, her face suffused with gratitude for his survival.

I had no idea what I'd do if I'd been in their position—if my son had been kidnapped and shot. All three of them had been wounded by gunshot, yet somehow, the mother and father had rallied enough strength from somewhere to stand there beside their little boy. In my line of work, I saw proof of how powerful mind over matter could be all the time. It never ever stopped short of amazing me.

I left the family behind and took my phone out as I walked out of the hospital room. "Tara? Damn. What does she want?" I mumbled to myself as I saw my ex-wife's name. Swiping the screen, I answered the call, bracing myself for what I knew would most likely be an enraging call. "Tara, what's up? You still picking up Eli around six tonight?"

"I can't," my ex said on the other end. I'd become used to hearing those words coming out of her mouth in the last two years since we'd divorced. "I've got plans that just came up."

"And they are?" I walked toward my office, needing some time to myself to process what the woman would tell me, and to figure out a way to let our son down yet again.

"Well, not that it's any of your business, but some of my girl-friends from the boutique want to take me out on the town tonight. To help get over the breakup."

"Get over?" She'd been dating this one guy for a little over six months—the longest relationship she'd had since our divorce. "You and Dale broke up?"

"He just wasn't meeting my needs." Tara had more than a handful of needs. I doubted anyone could meet them all. "You know what I mean, right?"

"Sure." No one knew better than I how much the woman needed.

"But I think you should spend this weekend with your son, and not on a drunken binge with those two giraffes who work for you at the boutique."

"I *need* this, Harman. You have no idea how swamped I've been with work this week." I doubted she'd personally lifted a perfectly manicured, fake-nailed finger at the shop. I'd bought the store for her as part of our divorce settlement, in the hopes that she could make some money on her own for a change. I knew that being hands-on had never been her style. "I had a sale on everything leopard print. It's time to let that look go to make room for the next hot thing, which is elephant prints, by the way."

That sounded hideous. "Do you know what kind of week *I've* had, Tara? Three tonsillectomies, two appendectomies, and I just had to remove a bullet from way too close to a little kid's spine..."

She laughed as she added, "And a partridge in a pear tree. Come on, Harman, you're used to doing those things. You actually love your work. I merely tolerate mine."

She'd begged for that damn shop. "You should love it. You gave me little choice but to fork over all the money you needed to make it work. See, Tara, that's one of your problems." She had so many they needed counting, but I didn't have the time for that. "You spend so much time focusing on the next thing you want, and then when you get it, you can't seem to focus on how happy it's made you. All you can do is find this thing and that thing wrong with it before you want to move onto something else."

"I'm so glad you brought that up, Harman," she sounded relieved for some reason. "I have such a great idea; I want to sell the boutique and buy a bar. Not just any bar, either. My bar will be like the hottest place in the city and everyone will totes want to go there."

Tara had always been shallow. After hiring a couple of girls in their young twenties to help out at her shop, it had just gotten worse. Now she tried to be hip and trendy—and it annoyed me to no end. "Tara, try to act your age. You're approaching thirty, you're not twenty-one anymore like the girls you hang out with. And need I remind you that you're also the mother of an eight-year-old boy?

That boy looks up to you. Don't you want to be a good role model for your son?"

"Me?" she scoffed. "Why do I need to do that when he has *you*, Harman. You're a pediatric surgeon, his Little League coach, and a billionaire to boot. That's enough to make you like a superhero or something to our son." She'd always thought that my accomplishments made up for her own shortcomings. "Just let me have this weekend to get over my loss of Dale, and I'll take one of your weekends when you have something you want to do. So like, ten years from now?" She laughed at her own lame joke as if the thought of me having plans was just too funny to think about.

Sure, I hadn't gone out much since the divorce—I was hard pressed to think of even one time I'd gone out in the last two years when it came down to it. But frankly, I had serious doubts about bringing any other woman around my son. I wanted to make sure any woman involved in my son's life was someone I could love and trust, and that was pretty difficult considering the fact that I'd never been in love before. Not even with the woman I'd married.

I'd met Tara at a nightclub nine years ago. With her long, shiny auburn hair, sleek legs, and tiny physique, she'd caught my eye. When I got close enough to really see her, I thought the light smattering of freckles across the bridge of her nose was cute. Foolishly, I thought her looks meant she was down to earth. I'd been wrong.

I'd also been wrong to assume the girl I'd asked to dance was over the age of twenty-one. We were at a nightclub for adults, after all. And I'd also been really wrong to have so much to drink. That lack in judgment had resulted in me being led by a girl I'd just met into the bathroom, where we'd proceeded to get it on—a thing that was totally out of character for me. I'd blamed the pink shots she'd kept making me buy for that poor decision.

Afterward, I could've just left her without so much as a goodbye, but I was a nice guy—for the most part. I'd given her my number and told her I'd had fun, and maybe we could do that again sometime.

Tara had taken the napkin I'd written my number on, folded it up neatly then tucked it under her drink while saying, "Thanks, I had fun, too. But you're really not my type. You're kind of...*old*."

I'd only been twenty-five and had assumed she was about that age as well. "*Old*? Since when is twenty-five considered old?"

"Ew!" she'd whined. "*That* old? I thought you were maybe twenty-three at the oldest. Yuck!"

"*Yuck*? If you didn't find me attractive, then why'd you go into that bathroom with me and do everything you'd done in there?" The girl had sucked me off before climbing onto my lap and riding me like a bucking bull.

"I mean, you're cute." She bit her bright-red lower lip. "And your body is like rock-hard, too." Her hands floated through the air as she ran them in front of me. I was wearing dress pants and a nice button-up, as I'd come from an event at the hospital I was doing my internship. "But you've got, like workingman's clothes on."

"And that *disgusts* you?" I couldn't figure her out at all.

Nodding, she went on, "Yeah. I want a college man. I'm not into some man-man, ya know?"

"Like a grown-ass man," I said with a nod, then ran my hand through my hair, feeling a little embarrassed that I'd actually screwed the girl before I'd even had a real conversation with her. "I'll get out of your way, so you can find yourself a little boy, then. I didn't realize you weren't into grown men." Her immaturity had me asking, almost as an after-thought, "How old are you, anyway?"

"Nineteen." She waved at a couple of girls who looked way older than she apparently was. "They got me into the club. They're my older brother's friends."

"Great." The regret didn't seem to end. It only got worse.

Three months later, I was sitting at the same bar, a beer in my hand after a particularly hard day—I'd observed a surgery where the doctor I'd shadowed had lost a little nine-year-old girl. "Hit me with a shot of Jack, will ya, Harvey?" The beer wasn't even coming close to cutting the pain down.

The front door opened and a bit of light streamed in. I held my hand over my eyes like a vampire who'd be burnt by the sun's rays.

"Thank God. I thought I'd never find you." When I opened my eyes at those words, I found Tara standing in the doorway and looking my way—only I'd forgotten her name at that time.

"Great." Talking to her had been the last thing I'd wanted to do. I took a long drink of my beer as the bartender placed the shot in front of me.

She pointed at the drink. "You should take that shot before you hear what I've got to tell you."

I remember thinking that whatever she had to tell me couldn't possibly make my day worse, but I followed her advice anyway. After pouring the searing hot liquor down my throat, I said, "Hit me."

Lifting her shirt, she ran her hand over the slightest little paunch on her otherwise flat stomach. "You're going to be a father. I lost your number and I'd forgotten your name."

My eyes were glued to that little bump and then they slowly crawled up her body, landing on her face. It was an okay face. Not the most gorgeous, but also not the ugliest I'd ever seen. Then I looked at the bartender, who'd become a statue as he looked at the girl with his mouth agape.

Chewing my lower lip, I weighed my options. Option one: give the chick a false name and leave Seattle for good. Option two: jump up and run like hell until I couldn't run anymore. Or option three: do the right thing—the way I'd been taught to.

Somewhere along the line in the next ten minutes, I went with my gut. "My name's Harman Hunter. And I've forgotten your name, too."

"Tara Flannigan." She finally put her shirt down. "My father would like to talk to you outside if you don't mind."

"Oh, shit," Harvey hissed.

I tended to agree with the bartender. "Yep." But I'd gotten up and faced the consequences of my actions like a real man. I'd married that girl and became the best husband and father I could be. And for six years, that'd been enough for Tara. Then when it wasn't anymore, she'd left. And not just me, but she'd left our son behind, too.

Her question pulled me out of my reverie, "Harman, so is it a go?"

"What?" I didn't fully understand her. "The bar, or the not-picking-up-Eli thing?"

"Well, for now, the not-picking-up-Eli thing," she clarified.

What else could I say? If I made her take him, then I had no idea what she'd do with him when she went out. Because she *would* still go out. "I'll come up with some excuse for you. Just try to think about being around more for your kid, okay?"

"Sure." She waited a beat. "And the bar?"

"Leave me out of that, please." I ended the call, wishing for the millionth time that I'd just worn a condom that fateful night. But then—as always—I took the wish back. I had no idea what I would do without my son. I loved that kid to the moon and back.

Though I'd made a lot of crappy decisions in my life, I could never think of my son as a mistake.

2

REBEL

THAT MOMENT I stumbled upon the beautiful early twentieth-century carriage house for sale in the prestigious Queen Anne neighborhood of Seattle, I knew it was mine. I am so damn proud of myself. It had been a hard few years, working to save enough money to make a down payment on a home, but after seeing the three-bedroom, two-bath, 2,000-square foot home, I knew it'd been worth it.

My first home!

If anyone had asked me back in the day if I'd be buying my own home at the tender age of twenty-five, I would've laughed until I cried. But there I was, doing just that.

The carriage house belonged to an estate that had just been inherited by a young woman who wanted to update the accompanying nineteenth-century mansion completely. The carriage house didn't fit into her scheme, so she sold it for a ridiculously low amount. Somehow, I'd been lucky enough to be one of the first to hear about it.

I'd been the vet on duty when a wounded pug came into the clinic after stepping on some glass during the demolition stage of the renovation. Beverly Song had inherited the place, and she and her three puppies were staying in the west wing while work began on the east side of the home. Poor little Pepper Pug had wandered over to the wrong side of the house and had gotten himself into trouble.

His unfortunate accident proved to be my great fortune as his owner told me all about the carriage house that just didn't fit into her plans. She'd already had a stone wall built around the back portion of the house to separate it permanently from her view. And she was just about to put it on the market.

No one else even had the chance to look at the place, as I'd called dibs immediately after she'd revealed the low price. I moved in only two short months later.

I had my furniture delivered and set up and then I got straight to working on my backyard. As a veterinarian, I liked to have animals around me all the time and living in an apartment hadn't allowed me to have any animals at all. Having my own home meant I could have anything I wanted—and I wanted to make sure I had things ready when I found my little pet guests.

Setting up some cages for various small animals, I also wanted to put up a kennel or two for any dogs I might find who needed help—or maybe even a new permanent home. But the kennel proved a bit hard to set up on my own, and I wasn't the only one who'd noticed.

"Hi, lady. You need some help?" I looked over my shoulder at the sound of a young boy's voice and found a kid in my backyard.

Brushing my hands over my jeans to clean them, I offered the kid a handshake. "Hi, I'm Rebel Saxe. Doctor Rebel Saxe. I'm a veterinarian—an animal doctor. What's your name?"

He shook my hand as he blew a chunk of thick auburn hair out of his dark-green eyes. "I'm Eli Hunter. My dad's a doctor, too. But he operates on little kids. So, are you going to have animals back here, Miss Saxe?"

I didn't much like having kids call me by my last name; it always made me feel old. "You can call me Rebel, Eli. And yes, I'm going to have all sorts of animals back here. Some will just be stopping by to recuperate here before going back into the wild, and some will be waiting for homes. Some will probably stay here forever with me, though."

"Cool." His eyes popped out of his head as he looked around the large yard. Then he wrinkled his little freckled nose. "How're you gonna take care of them all?"

"I don't know." He'd hit a point I hadn't taken a look at yet. I knew I had more cages and space set up than my free time would allow. "I suppose I'll just have to make time for them, won't I?"

"I could help ya." He shoved his hands in the pockets of his blue jeans, grinning up at me. "I live right next door, and I'm not busy most of the time. I could help ya. I like animals—even though I don't have none yet."

The place next door was an enormous and gorgeous estate with a monstrous house. I expected the boy came from a rich family who might not want him working at all. "I'd love your help, but what will your parents think about that?"

"Dad wouldn't care. He likes helping people; he always tells me I should, too." He followed my gaze, looking toward his house. "We weren't always this rich, you know."

I didn't think it was right to be getting into the family's finances with this little boy. "Oh, you don't have to explain anything to me."

"No, I want to!" Eli brushed his hair back with all the impatience of a kid his age, as that pesky chunk had fallen back into his eyes. "Dad saved this little girl's life a couple years ago, and her dad had lots of money. He gave my dad a bunch of it, and Dad made something he called 'vestments,' and now he's got billions and billions. So he bought us a fancy house, and he's got more cars than I can count."

"How nice for your family." I smiled at his enthusiasm as he told the story and at what I thought must've been a couple of exaggerations. It also floated across my mind how nice it would be to save a rich person's pet and get the same type of gift. Though I was happy enough to have saved a rich person's pet and gotten a great deal on a house.

"Yeah, it is pretty nice being rich. I 'member I used to have to wait for my birthday or Christmas to get 'spensive things. Now, I just tell Dad what I want, and most of the time he gets it for me. But sometimes he don't. Sometimes he says I should wait for a special occasion. Like, I been askin' for a dog for a while now, and he keeps saying, 'let's wait on that, Little Buddy.' He calls me his little buddy on account of I am his buddy. We do lots of things together. I think I might be his best friend."

I thought that sounded sweet. His energetic rambling was infectious. "And is he *your* best friend, Eli?"

Shaking his head, he said, "Nah. I like playing with Jason from my class. I'm in the second grade this year, and we sit next to each other. He's funny and makes me laugh a lot, so that makes him my best friend."

"I'm sure your father doesn't mind sharing you with him." I looked back at my half-made kennel and thought the boy might be of some help. "I could sure use another set of hands if you're not too busy to help me out for a minute."

The smile that broke out over his face told me that was just what he'd been hoping to hear. "Sure, Rebel! I can help."

"If you can hold this metal piece right here, then I can pull the wire straight and attach it to the other one I've managed to get set up." I pulled on my end while he held fast to his and in no time we'd put the kennel up.

Standing back, we both had smiles on our faces. "We did it, Rebel!"

The kid deserved something for his hard work. "I think this calls for a celebration. I've got cookies and milk inside. You want me to grab us some?" I nodded toward the small outdoor table and chairs. "If you'll have a seat, I'll bring them out. I doubt your parents would approve of you going into a stranger's house."

"I bet you're right." He said as he walked over to the table and sat down. "My dad might get upset with me."

I noticed he'd only spoken about his father. "And what about your mother?" I felt bad about prying, but figured I was hardly the first person in the world who wanted to get to know her neighbors.

"She wouldn't find out, not with her being all the way over at her house." Sliding into the chair, I noticed a frown on his face. "She was supposed to get me for this weekend, but she called Dad and said she can't make it. She's working at her shop."

The disappointment in his face tore at my heart. "Well, I'm sure she's very busy, or else she would've picked you up."

"She mostly doesn't," he said as he looked at the table, running his finger over the floral design. "I haven't seen her in lots of days. I talk to her every day on my cell phone, though." He pulled it out of his pocket. "Dad gave me this when Mom left. He told me I could talk to her as much as I wanted to with this phone."

"He sounds like a great dad." Though I knew nothing else about the man, it was clear he did the best he could with his son.

"Yeah, he's pretty good." He looked at the French doors that led into the back of my new house. "Can I have water 'stead of milk? I'm lactose intolerant, and milk gives me the squirty poops."

A laugh burst out of me. "Sorry, that's rude of me. Sure, I'll get you water instead. I'll be right back."

As I grabbed the box of cookies and a couple bottles of water, I wondered about the kid's life. Sure, they had a great place to live, and it sounded like his dad had a great job, but what kind of family life did the boy have?

When I went back outside, I put some napkins down, then handed him a bottle of water. "Here you go, Eli." I took a seat, then opened the box of cookies. "I sure feel lucky to have met you."

"I feel lucky, too." He took a bite of the cookie. "Yum. Did you make these homemade, Rebel?"

"No. A girl at work gave them to me this afternoon before I left the clinic. She thought I should have something to munch on while I moved into my home." I looked around my backyard and my heart swelled full of emotion. "This is the very first house I've bought on my own." Looking back at him, I tousled his hair. "Sure am glad to have a great neighbor like you, Eli. I think we'll be great friends."

"I think so, too." He smiled at me, showing off his missing front tooth before he looked down and tried to get the lid off the water.

Reaching over, I unscrewed it for him. "There ya go."

"Thanks." He took a drink. "Maybe, since we live next to an animal doctor now, my dad will let me get a dog."

"Well, even if he doesn't, you can always come over here and play with the animals I'll have here—especially if you're going to help me out some." I thought I should make him a definite deal. "How about I pay you twenty dollars a week to come over here every evening when I get home from work? You can help me feed the animals—it shouldn't take more than a few minutes—and then you could play with them if you'd like."

"I've gotta ask my dad, but *my* answer is yes!" His bright green eyes shone as he grinned. "He'll probably want to come over to meet you."

Pushing my hand through my hair, I hoped I didn't look too much a mess after the work I'd done, and I wondered about the boy's father. "Well, if he's busy, we can meet another time." If he were busy, I'd get a chance to clean myself up before meeting the man.

"Nah, he's not busy at all. He was working out in the gym at our house. He does that a lot." He took out his cell and made the call.

I sat there picturing what a man who worked out a lot in his home gym must look like. Then I ran my hand through my hair again. "I'm just gonna pop into my house for a sec. You wait here, okay?"

He nodded as I headed inside to freshen up a little. Meeting anyone new while wearing a sweaty t-shirt and cut-off shorts was not ideal, and it definitely wasn't the way I wanted to introduce myself to any of my new neighbors. You only get one chance at a first impression, after all.

3

HARMAN

THE RINGING of my cell signaled the end of my workout. Wiping the sweat off my face, I walked over to check the caller and found it was my son, Eli. Last I'd seen, he'd been in the foyer, watching something out the front window. "Hey, Eli. What's up?"

"Dad, I'm over at the new neighbor's house. The little one in front of the big one that weird lady is making into a big mess—you know the one, right?" he asked.

Alarm bells immediately started clanging in my head. My son was way too trusting. "First, why did you leave our place without telling me? Second, what are you doing, going to stranger's houses? Third, why are you calling me when you know you should be getting your backside home?"

"She's nice, Dad," he told me. "She's a vet—you know, an animal doctor. And she wants to give me a job."

"I don't think that's a good idea, Eli." He was just a little boy, who would want to put him to work? And what kind of job could he do for anyone? "Come on home, son."

"Dad, just come meet her, and then you'll see it's going to be great for me," he sounded enthusiastic. "Come on. Please, Dad."

That little pleading voice always got to me. And I'd been meaning to introduce myself to the new neighbor anyway. "I'll be there in a few minutes."

The woman who'd inherited the house next to ours had been doing all kinds of renovations and downright demolishing other structures on the property. The rock wall behind the carriage house had gone up not too long ago, for what I now realized must have been to separate the two houses and properties. It sounded like some retired veterinarian—maybe an old widow—had moved into the place. Perhaps she wanted Eli to help feed her cats or something. I supposed it wouldn't hurt anything for him to help out the elderly a bit.

Jogging out the door, I figured I'd do a little cool-down from my workout while heading over to the place. I didn't bother changing out of my workout clothes, thinking this would be a short visit. I'd say hello, tell her it was nice to meet her. Let her know, sure, Eli could feed her cats, and then it'd be goodbye. No need to change clothes for that.

I saw Eli standing in the front yard when I got out onto the street. He waved his arms real big, as if there was any chance I couldn't see him standing there. "Over here, Dad."

"I see you." I chuckled as I jogged up to him. "So, where is she?"

"Come on, she's around back. Or she will be." He led me around the side of the house. "She went inside for a minute. She'll be right back."

I saw a few cages and a kennel in the backyard. "Looks like she's going to have quite a few animals back here. Are you sure you can handle being responsible for her pets, Eli?"

"She's gonna be 'sponsible for them, too, Dad." He pointed at the double French doors at the back of the house. "There she is."

Looking up, I caught sight of a very lovely brunette coming our way. Faded blue jeans hugged her legs, showing off some pretty great assets. Her tight t-shirt clung to what I figured were D cups, at least. And that smile she wore—that smile alone could light up the dark quite easily.

"Hi." She extended her hand. "I'm Doctor Rebel Saxe."

Shaking her hand, I nearly forgot my own name, "I...um, I'm—"

"This is my dad," Eli saved the day. "His name's Harman."

Moving her hand out of mine, she gestured to a small outdoor table. "Care for some cookies, Harman?"

My tongue felt like it weighed a ton, and my brain didn't seem to be working at all. But it did manage to make my feet work, walking me over to the table and chairs she'd pointed to. We all sat down, and Eli took over. "So, Dad, Rebel wants me to help her out, and she's gonna pay me twenty bucks a week!"

That jarred me back to reality and had me shaking my head. I didn't think she needed to pay him. "No. That's okay."

Rebel's pretty blue eyes—eyes the color of a bluebird's wings— went to Eli. "I'm sorry, sport. But if your dad doesn't want you to do this, then that's that."

That wasn't *that* at all. "No. I mean you don't have to pay him. It's the neighborly thing to do, right?"

Now she shook her head. "I can't let him work for free." She looked at me with a smile. "Your son told me you're a doctor. He said you work with kids."

"Yeah, I'm a pediatric surgeon at Saint Christopher's General Hospital." Finally, my brain was thawing out. "And he said you're a vet. Where is it you work?"

"I work over at A Place for Paws Clinic." She looked at Eli. "Your son's been telling me how much he's been wanting a dog of his own. I figure he'll enjoy helping me with the animals I bring home."

"I see." I looked at my son and wondered when he got to be such a chatterbox. "Well, you can't have a dog of your own. Not yet. But if you prove to me that you can be responsible for animals, that'll be a big feather in your cap."

Eli jumped up and clapped his hands, and I found myself smiling. I hadn't seen him that happy in a very long time. "Thanks, Dad!" He pointed at the kennel. "I helped Rebel put that up already. I can be a big help to her."

Looking back at the young woman, I couldn't help but wonder

why my son had been the one to help her out. "Did you move into this place all on your own?"

Nodding, she leaned back in her chair then picked up a bottle of water off the table. "This is my first home."

"Seems you're quite accomplished. A vet and a home owner, and you can't be more than what? Twenty-four?" It seemed she was a driven young woman. "That's something to be proud of."

Her cheeks went pink with a blush. It didn't look like she wore any makeup at all, and yet she still looked radiant. "I'm twenty-five, actually, and I'm a little bit of an overachiever. My mother started homeschooling me because I got bored in regular classes. They went too slow for me. I graduated high school when I was only fifteen. Then I went to college. And college courses, I liked. Not long into that, I found a calling in the veterinarian world, and now I'm here—a real vet with my own home. Feels like all my dreams have come true."

"Impressive." I wasn't just blowing smoke either—the woman really had impressed me. "I think Eli working with you is a great idea. It seems like you'd be a great role model for him."

She looked at Eli with affection in her eyes—clearly she didn't only have a soft spot for animals, but for nosy eight-year-olds, too. "He's a great kid, from what I can see so far. It would be my pleasure to get to spend time with him." Reaching over, she tousled his hair. "I'll teach you all kinds of things about animals, Eli. It'll be fun."

"I think so, too!" Eli looked at me. "I'm glad Mom didn't come get me this weekend. Rebel might've given the job to another kid, and I would've missed out."

I looked down, not really wanting to discuss my mess of an ex in front of our new neighbor. A woman like her, one who looked like she had it all going on, would never have time for something as messy as my life.

Rebel waded into the depths of my complicated relationship anyway. "Eli, I don't want you turning down spending time with your mother just to help me." She darted a quick glance my way, as if to gauge my reaction. "It's important to make time for the people you love."

"Yes, ma'am." Eli looked at me. We both knew that his mother was the one who wasn't making the time for him, not the other way around, as Rebel implied. "Maybe *you* should tell Mom what Rebel said. Maybe then she'll see how important I am."

Putting my hand on his shoulder, I looked him in the eyes. "You *are* important to her, Eli. Don't let it get into your head that you're not. She's just very busy with her business." Sure, it was a lie, but someone had to safeguard the poor kid from his mother's neglect.

Rebel gently put her hand on his other shoulder. "See, I told you she must be very, very busy to have missed out on spending time with you."

Seemed my kid had told the woman a hell of a lot personal information. "Yes, Tara's a very busy woman," I tried to make it sound legitimate. "She owns a boutique, and she's only had it for about a year. It takes a lot of time to get something like that going strong. She's only getting alimony for eight more years, so she has to find some way to support herself before that time runs out."

Rebel nodded. "Well, I hope she has good luck with that. I'm sure running a business isn't easy. It's not something I'd like to do. Not yet, anyway."

Eli's expression told me he didn't think his mother was working all that hard. "Well, maybe she works harder when I'm not around. Whenever I go to the store, she just talks on the phone the whole time."

Rebel looked at me briefly before her eyes returned to Eli. "You know, with a job like hers, she probably has to be on the phone a lot. She has to order things for her shop and everything. We have to do that at the clinic sometimes, and we hardly sell any products at all."

I had to hand it to the woman, she was certainly trying her best to make Tara sound good. I knew that was *not* the case, but I appreciated that she was looking out for my son's feelings.

Wanting nothing more than to get off the subject of my son's mother, I asked, "So do you specialize in any specific field of veterinary medicine, Rebel?"

"I do." Her face glowed, and I could tell she had a passion for her work. "I've got a thing for miniature animals. Not that I agree with the breeding practices that make them, but I do believe that people need to have a better understanding of these breeds than they currently do. There are so many problems with miniatures—from digestion, to breathing, and even eyesight and hearing. I'm working to develop ways to help these tiny creatures live better lives."

Eli seemed pumped about that. "So, a lot of the animals you'll be bringing home are gonna be tiny?"

"Most will be, yes." She beamed at him. "Do you like little animals?"

"Who doesn't?" Eli got up and went to one of the small cages. "So, what kind of animal can fit into this cage?"

"All kinds. We could have some baby skunks or possums that have been left alone after something happens to their mothers, or maybe some piglets. Those things are all the rage right now."

Looking at the kennel, I had to ask as curiosity bid me. "You could fit one of those mini ponies in that thing, couldn't you?"

"I could." She nodded. "But I don't like to keep animals of that sort in such small enclosures. I don't think I've got enough room here to take in any of those types of animals anyway."

"Yeah," I said as I looked around at the posh neighborhood. "Barnyard animals might not be welcomed around here."

"Most likely not." Rebel looked at the rock wall at the back of her yard. "I don't think Beverly Song would like that, either. She's got some definite opinions of what she wants to see and doesn't want to see, and I'm not trying to make her mad. I never in a million years thought I'd be living in the Queen Anne neighborhood. I don't want to be run out of here for having a bunch of noisy, smelly animals."

I'd only lived in the place a little under two years, so I understood what she meant. "Wait until your first HOA meeting. They really know how to throw a party around here. Caviar and champagne are staples at those things."

Eli put his finger in his mouth, mock-gagging. "Yuck."

"I'm with you. I hate both those nasty things," Rebel agreed.

"So, no champagne for you then, Rebel?" I figured her for a fancy cocktail drinker.

"No, thank you. When I do drink, I prefer Jack and Coke."

Now that's my kind of girl.

4

REBEL

THE MAN SITTING across the table didn't look anything like his son. Harman had sandy blonde hair and green eyes, but his weren't anywhere near the dark shade of Eli's. Harman's were more like a sea-green—kind of dreamy—sexy, even.

He'd come over wearing loose-fitting black shorts and a t-shirt with the arms cut out. Even if Eli hadn't already clued me in, it would've been obvious that Harman had just come from his workout —his tanned skin still glowed from the sweat he'd worked up.

Every visible muscle was toned and perfectly formed. From his shoulders to his ankles, it was clear that the man took care of his body.

I wasn't the kind to work out in a gym. I got the majority of my exercise at work, lifting heavy animals and chasing after runaway pets whenever necessary.

"Speaking of the neighborhood, there's a sweet place to run a few blocks over." Harman jerked his head in the direction he meant. "I could show you sometime if you'd like. It's well-lit and perfect for early morning runs."

"Do you usually run in the mornings?" I barely made it out of bed and to the shower before going to work.

"Every day that it's not raining—which, in Seattle, isn't often. That's why I have the home gym." He looked in the direction of his place. "You're welcome to work out in it any time you want. I'll leave your name with the maid, and she'll let you in whenever you want."

"That's very nice of you." It seemed I was getting off on the right foot with my neighbor, but I wasn't sure if I we were quite on those terms yet. "I wouldn't want to go into your home when you're not there, though. And to be honest, I don't exercise much, other than what I do at work. Which is a lot."

"Well, the morning run then?" he asked, seeming hopeful.

"The only running I do in the morning is to the coffee maker before running to get into a hot shower." I knew I sounded lazy, but it was the truth.

Still trying to get me on the exercise train, he put in another offer. "Well, Eli and I have a little nightly routine you might enjoy."

Eli clapped and hopped up and down. "Oh, yeah! Me and Dad swim in the indoor pool every night at eight o'clock on the dot. We have races and do laps around the big pool. You could come!"

Harman added, "It does wonders for a good night's rest." His smile—and the image of him in a bathing suit—did things to me that were dangerous. "I could leave the golf cart at the gate for you if you don't want to walk all that way."

"How generous of you both." I didn't know what to say. It felt rude to turn down everything they offered. "I suppose I'd like to give that a try. It sounds like it would be a great way to wind down after a long day. How long do you guys swim for, anyway?"

"An hour," Harman told me.

My mouth dropped open. "You swim—nonstop—for an entire hour?"

He nodded as Eli shouted, "Sure we do! And then we get out, take a quick shower and get into bed, and I fall right to sleep almost 'mediately too."

"You both sound like pros." I knew I could never keep up with either of them. It surprised me that little Eli could even keep up with his dad. "Do you always exercise with your dad?"

"Nah. He won't let me lift weights and stuff yet. He says it'll stunt my growth. But I run with him sometimes on the weekends. He gets up too early for me to go with him on school days." Eli walked around to pat his dad on the back. "Plus, his legs are longer, so he runs faster than me. I slow him down when I go with him."

"I don't mind, Little Buddy." Harman ran his hand through his son's thick auburn hair. "We need to stop and see the barber Monday on our way home from school. I hadn't realized how shaggy you've gotten."

"I could give him a trim." I'd taken some cosmetology classes in college before setting my sights on veterinary school, but then remembered that I hadn't finished unpacking yet. "After I unpack tomorrow, that is. I keep forgetting about all the work I need to do inside."

"And we're getting in your way of that," Harman said a little sheepishly. "I'm sorry. We'll get out of your hair, Rebel."

"Actually, I needed to take a break anyway." I'd worked hard for several hours, and if Eli hadn't come by, I would've worked right through dinner without even eating. "There's no rush to leave. I won't be getting back to work until after dinner anyway. I keep trying to remind myself that I've got the entire weekend to get everything put away. No reason to hurry and wear myself out completely."

"Maybe you shouldn't swim tonight then," Eli said, thoughtfully. "That might be too much for you, Rebel."

I laughed as I looked at Harman. "He's such a sweet kid. You've raised him well."

"Thanks." Harman looked at his son out of the corner of his eyes, and I could see it written all over his handsome face. He felt sad about something.

My bets were on the absent mother and how she'd let down their son. "Would you like a bottle of water, Harman?"

He turned his head and smiled at me. "I'd actually love one. I should've grabbed one before leaving the house but didn't count on hanging out here so long."

Eli was standing beside his dad and quickly offered to get that sorted. "I'll get him one. Can I go inside your house, Rebel?"

"Yep. The kitchen is right there, and the water is in the fridge. Ignore the cluttered countertops, please." I'd yet to put the kitchen stuff away.

"Sure." He took off, and I found Harman looking at him as he went.

"So, wanna tell me about your ex?" I wasn't usually so nosy, but it felt like the elephant in the room at that point. I figured I might as well open that door, knowing that he likely wouldn't, even though a certain amount of sadness radiated off him.

"Is it that obvious?" he chuckled. "Am I *that* guy now? The one who everyone can tell is having a hard time with his life?"

"You most likely don't radiate it as much as you are right now, around your son." I hoped that softened the blow. "You're hurting for that boy, I can tell."

"His mother wasn't ever the greatest, but she did try to be motherly and do things for him while we were together." He leaned back in the chair, then looked up. "She was young when we married. Nineteen, to be exact. And pregnant. And we weren't in love at all."

"A shotgun wedding?" I had to ask. "People still do that sort of thing?"

"In my family we did. I was brought up to know what it means to take care of the people in my life." He looked at me. "You know...do what's right?"

"So, she got pregnant, and you did what was right." It was respectable, even if it wasn't the smartest thing to do. "And how old were you?"

"Twenty-five." He smiled. "Your age now. I'm thirty-three now, just so you know."

I nodded. "I figured you were around that age." Realizing how that sounded, I got a little flustered. "Not that I was looking that hard at you."

"I'm sure you weren't." He flexed one bicep, and my eyes went straight to it.

We both started laughing. "Okay, maybe I *was* looking a little. But you've got to admit that you've built a pretty impressive body there, Doctor Hunter."

"And he even told you our last name?" he groaned as he shook his head. "I swear I don't know what's gotten into that kid. He's never been so chatty in his life."

I didn't know why the boy felt like he could talk to me, but I liked it. "Maybe he's missing an older female to talk to. How long's it been since he's seen his mother? He told me he can't count all the days it's been."

"Shit." Harman's head dropped. "I try not to count the days myself. I think it's been about three weeks."

"That's a long time to a little kid," I remembered the first time I went away to spend a week at my grandparents' house. "When I was ten, I went away from home for a week. I swear, I thought the whole summer had passed by while I was away. It seemed like forever. I can't imagine how he feels."

I saw his shoulders droop at that, and it made me feel awful for what I'd said. The man clearly already felt awful about the situation; he didn't need me to rub it in.

"I can't, either," he confided. "I don't miss his mother at all. Mostly because our marriage had been over for a long time before she left. Funny how she decided she wanted to end things only after I started making a tidy sum of money."

"Ah, alimony." I nodded, understanding how those things could happen. "So, do you look at that like a good side effect of getting that generous gift from your patient's father or a bad one?"

He lifted his head and our eyes met. "He told you about our financials, too?"

I nodded and had to laugh at his bewildered expression. "Yep. I guess he trusts me for some reason."

"Wow." He blinked a few times. "Well, first off, let me say that the money wasn't an outright gift, and it didn't happen because of my work. It's not entirely ethical for physicians to take huge amounts of money from their patients' families just for doing our jobs, and I wouldn't have taken it if I could've avoided it. But this money was all tied up in investments and stock shares, and I couldn't exactly refuse it, so I figured I'd make the most of it.

"Now, as for my ex—for me personally, her leaving was good. But for our son, it wasn't. It's like she washed her hands of Eli when she washed her hands of me, and he doesn't deserve that. I did—I didn't love her. That's why I haven't fought her on much of anything since the divorce. She could have Eli any time she wants, but she won't even take him when the custody papers say she can. I gave him a cell phone, so they could talk as much as they wanted, but she only answers his calls once a day. And those always end with her telling him she's got work to do and can't talk to him for longer."

It sounded like the woman had many faults, but I couldn't help but empathize with her—it couldn't have been easy to have a baby so young. Before I could stop myself, I was voicing my opinion. "I'm sure she just doesn't realize the impact she's having on your son. Having a baby that young might make a woman feel like she's missed out on a lot of things. Have you brought her attention to it?"

"I have." He looked at me with those sad eyes. "She's not working this weekend. She's getting drunk with her friends to get over the latest guy she just dumped. I did tell her how important it is to spend time with her son, but she was hell-bent on going. And when that woman sets her mind on something she wants, there's really no stopping her."

"Oh, that sounds...rough." I'd clearly butted in where I didn't belong. I'd never dealt with family troubles before, and though I wished I could help Eli—that enthusiastic boy deserved to be happy —I was out of my depth. I'd been there for families who had lost a pet or were losing one, but humans losing humans wasn't my forte. "Perhaps a counselor would help her?" That seemed like some solid advice.

"She won't go to one." He smiled weakly. "As a doctor, that was my go-to suggestion. I took Eli to one for a little while when we first separated, but Tara turned any family or individual counseling down flat.

I'm not sure who or what could get through to her at this point. I just wish my son could have his mother back. That's all I really want."

"If she decided she wanted to come back, would you let her?" It wasn't my business at all, but I felt the man was getting desperate.

"I might. I might let her come back if it meant she started being there for our son again." He looked up as Eli came out with the water. "But I don't want her back for me. I'm over our marriage completely."

At least he wasn't pining away for the woman, and I couldn't say I blamed him for moving on so easily. The man had that—and a whole lot else—going for him.

5

HARMAN

I HADN'T FELT SO at ease with a woman in a very long time. There was a genuineness to Rebel that just radiated from her. There didn't seem to be even one fake thing about her. And that seemed to be only one great quality among many about the woman. And it didn't hurt that she was absolutely gorgeous.

"Dad, here's your water." Eli put the bottle in front of me, then took a seat at the table, turning his attention to Rebel after barely glancing my way. "You sure got lots to do in there."

Nodding, she said, "I do. But I've got all weekend to do it. I'm going to go grab something for dinner and eat before I get back to work." Her eyes moved to mine. "Where's the best place to get a veggie burger around here?"

And there it was—her one flaw. "You're a vegetarian?"

"Lord, no." She laughed, and the way her eyes sparkled made my crotch ache. "It's just that I've found if a place can make something like that taste good, then they usually make one hell of a great burger."

Relief washed over me. "Well, that's good to hear. For a second there, I thought we couldn't be friends."

Her laughter made me smile, and I felt a little flip in my chest, in an area suspiciously close to my heart. "Vegetarians are off limits, huh?"

Romantically speaking, no one was really off limits unless they didn't get along with my son. And I had no idea why I was thinking romantically about this woman I'd barely met. I needed to get off the subject.

"There isn't a good burger place around here. As you can imagine, the people who live around here tend to like things that are a bit more upscale. There are a lot of fancy bistros and cafes, but burgers aren't really their thing. But I happen to have a chef who can make some pretty good ones. Why don't you come over and eat dinner with us?"

"Yeah!" Eli shouted, his fist pumping into the air. "Come on, Rebel. I want to show you around our mansion."

I'd told him not to call our home that. If it'd been up to me, we would be living in something much smaller. But Tara had insisted on the sprawling home, and Eli loved the place so much I couldn't bring myself to make him move now that Tara's opinion didn't matter.

"Eli, it's just our home. I don't like you putting on airs like that." Looking at Rebel, I apologized, "Sorry about that. He's just a kid who hasn't always lived this sort of life. It shows on him sometimes."

"I understand, and I don't see anything wrong with what he said." She reached over and patted him on the shoulder. "If I lived in a mansion, I'd be pretty happy about it, too."

Eli nodded. "We went from a tiny apartment to something that's bigger than the museum I went to once on a field trip in kindergarten. I think it's cool. We got a room with a pool table and one with a piano. We don't know how to play it, but it's there."

"The previous owner left a few things behind," I told her. "So, will you come for dinner?"

"I shouldn't impose on you like that—not when we've just met." She looked down at her hands in her lap, seeming shy for the first time.

"I don't know what that means," Eli said, "but you should come. Please."

She smiled at the pleading tone of his voice that got to me so easily. "Okay. ...if you're sure. I'd love to join you guys for dinner tonight. And once I get all settled, you two will have to join me for dinner one night and let me cook you my famous lasagna."

"Deal," I said quickly, and then pulled out my cell. "Let me text Rene about the burgers, and then we'll head over."

Rebel looked toward my place. "Should I take my car? I don't want to walk home in the dark."

I thought about how nice it would be to walk her home, to get a little more time with her without Eli tagging along. "I'll make sure I get you back here safe and sound. There are tons of lights in this neighborhood—you'll have a hard time finding many shadows around here. I'll walk you home afterward."

"How nice of you." Rebel got up as I stood. "Looks like I've found myself a couple of gentlemen. Let me just lock up."

Eli ran ahead of us as we walked side by side out of her backyard. "There's really no need for that. There are too many security cameras around here to worry about anyone taking anything. You're in a very safe place. But do lock your doors at night. It's just safer that way."

"That's good to know." We headed up the street, and she looked up the long drive to my place. "It must've felt so weird when you moved from a little apartment to this place."

"We all felt out of place for a while." I thought about how Tara had griped about the new neighborhood almost instantly. Typical Tara, finding something to complain about even though she'd gotten exactly what she'd demanded in the first place. "Tara only managed to stay a few months here before she left. She kept saying she couldn't take the way people around here looked down their noses at her."

"So, I suppose that's something I'll have to endure as a mere peasant living in a carriage house meant to house the help." The way she laughed as she spoke told me she didn't much care about that.

"It helps to keep a good attitude about it, I've found." I hadn't encountered the resistance Tara had whined about. "Most of these people are nice. You have to understand where they came from, with most of them coming from long lines of money. And then you've got the bougie rich—the new rich people who like to pretend they've come from old money. And then there's me. Just a lucky guy who happened to be in the right place at the right time and came into a bunch of money for it."

"What happened with that whole thing? It all sounds rather extraordinary," she asked as we headed up my driveway.

"Eli and I were in New York. I was to attend a seminar and took him with me. One of my aunts lives there, so she watched him for me while I was at the conference." I could still remember the smells in the air that day. "I spotted a hot dog vendor, and I told Eli we should get a real New York hot dog. We were standing in the line when a man in an expensive suit walked by with his little girl, who had a hot dog in her hand. She'd taken a bite of it already, and I saw the look on her face just as the thing lodged in her throat. She fell to the ground, and her father had no idea what was wrong with her. He started to panic."

"And you sped into action, didn't you?" Eyes wide, she looked a little amazed.

I'd never thought of what I did as heroic in any way. Compared to what I did at work every day, giving someone the Heimlich is really no big deal. And I always thought if I hadn't been there, then someone else would've helped the poor kid—it just happened to look more impressive that there was a doctor on the scene.

"I told him she was choking on the hot dog, scooped her up and then dislodged the food fairly easily. And just like that, I'd earned the man's undying gratitude. He got my name, number, and address before we parted ways, and I didn't really think anything of it."

"How long did it take before you knew about his reward?" She pushed a chunk of shiny, dark hair out of her face as a gust of wind blew it out of place.

"A week." I reached out to move another stray lock of hair, tucking it behind her ear. "I received a phone call from the man's attorney. He was in Seattle and asked if he could come to my home. He came over and told me that the man had given me a ton of shares in his company—his very successful multibillion-dollar company—along with some other investments. He also brought a gift bag with keys to a new BMW that he'd parked outside of our little apartment, a couple of Rolex watches, and some other things that were also incredibly expensive. I refused the smaller gifts, but the shares and all the money that went along with them weren't as easy to turn away."

Whistling, she said, "What a surprise that must've been."

"As a doctor yourself, you can imagine the kind of student loan debt I was in. Just being able to pay that off was more than I could've ever wanted." I wondered how she'd take the rest of the story. "I took some of the shares and sold them, using that money to make more investments. I chose a very good investment firm to handle that, and in the matter of just one year, I'd doubled my money. And this last year, I quadrupled it.

"It all happened so fast and under such wild circumstances that it doesn't feel right sometimes. So a couple months ago, I set up a scholarship fund that'll pay off the student loans of other doctors who win contests I come up with. And the best part is that I've got it set up so the interest off another account keeps that account at a constant amount of a couple hundred million, so I can keep on helping my fellow doctors all around the world."

Rebel reached out to put her hand on my shoulder, staring at me with the strangest expression—not quite awe, and something approaching a seriousness I hadn't yet seen in her. "Harman, that's truly noble of you." She blinked a few times. "You've had a pretty remarkable life."

"You could definitely say that. But I think most people would do the same thing if they were in my shoes—nothing too noble about it." I started walking again. I always felt embarrassed telling people my story, and I didn't want her to make a big thing out of it.

"I don't think so." She came along, staying at my side. "But I can see you're not comfortable with the praise. I'll try to hold back my accolades."

I had to laugh at that—she just had a way of making me feel comfortable, even when talking about the subjects that made me most uncomfortable. First with Tara, now with this. I couldn't help but feel at ease—even happy—in her presence. "Yes, please try to hold them back. I'm not used to people saying such nice things about me."

Her brows shot up as her expression turned to surprise. "Really?" she asked in disbelief. "Have you forgotten that you're a doctor?" I found myself laughing at her again—she was right, I did hear a lot of compliments and gratitude in my field of work, but that wasn't what I was referring to, and she seemed to pick up on that. "Who knows about what you're doing? And who hasn't told you how great it is?"

"Other than the people at the investment firm and my bank, you're the only one who knows about the scholarship fund so far." I didn't know exactly why I'd even told her. "I haven't come up with a contest yet, so I've been waiting to figure that out before announcing it. But I'll come up with one very soon. I'm eager to get this going."

"Oh, how about an essay contest?" she suggested after a brief pause. "You can ask people to send you their stories about why they wanted to become a doctor in the first place. Then the winner can be the one that hits you in the heart the hardest."

"That would mean a lot of reading, wouldn't it?" I nudged her shoulder with mine. "I might need someone's help for all that."

"You'd let me help you?" she asked, seeming stunned.

"Why not? It's your idea." I looked up at the front door and stepped up to open it for her. "And now, to show off my cook's skills." I stepped to one side to allow her to go in ahead of me. "After you."

Eli laughed as he ran in a circle behind us. "Dad, you're silly."

Rebel looked at me with shining eyes. "I think you're extremely nice—and hardly silly at all." Her shoulder brushed my chest as she moved past me. And at the brief touch, I lost my breath, my train of thought, and maybe even a little bit of my heart.

6

REBEL

THAT EVENING with Harman and Eli bordered on magical. I'd always gotten along well with people, whether I'd known them a long time or had just met them. But the way I meshed with Eli and his father felt different. It felt as if they'd always been a part of my life—almost as if I belonged with those two.

Perhaps because they both felt the loss of the wife and mother role in their lives, they were reaching out to me far more than anyone ever had before. There was this look in their eyes that told me they were missing something—or maybe just needed a feminine ear to hear what they had to say.

All I knew for sure was that when Saturday and Sunday came around and neither of them had stopped by my place, I felt a bit lost. But then at six o'clock on Sunday evening, there was a knock at my front door. I'd just finished putting away the last of my things and settled down in my recliner with a much-needed Jack and Coke.

Thinking it might have been the last of some of the new décor items I'd ordered being delivered, I was surprised when I opened the door to find the two guys I'd been missing standing there. Harman had a basket of fruit in his hands, and Eli had a stunning crystal vase full of the deepest red roses I'd ever seen. "Welcome to the neighborhood," Harman said with a smile.

"I thought you guys might've forgotten about me." I stepped back to let them in.

"Dad said we should give you time to put your things away." Eli scanned the living room, nodding approvingly. "And it looks like you've got things put away now."

"I've just finished the last little bit. I'm pretty much completely moved in and ready to sit back and relax for the rest of the evening." It felt good to have everything done and even better to have them visiting me.

Harman put the basket of fruit on the coffee table. "This looks pretty good right here. Eli, put the flowers on the bar over there." A long bar ran between my living room and kitchen, separating the two.

"Thank you, guys. This is really sweet of you both." I took a seat in my recliner, not reclining in it the way I'd planned. "Sit down and tell me how your weekend went."

"It's been fine, uneventful," Harman replied as he and Eli took seats on either end of the sofa. "You feel like grabbing some dinner with us? I always give the chef Sunday's off."

That sounded wonderful to me. "You sure?"

Eli jumped up, his hands in the air. "Yeah, we're sure. We're going to that pizza place that has all the games, and it'll be lots of fun."

Once again, the little boy's enthusiasm had a smile spreading across my face. "I've got to admit, that sounds awesome. It's been ages since I've done anything like that."

Eli came to take my hands. "Then let's go!"

"I've gotta go grab my purse." I said, getting up and heading to my bedroom to grab my things.

When I came back into the living room, I noticed that Eli had already left, and Harman stood near the door, waiting for me. "The kid's excited to have you joining us."

I wondered if he was excited, too, but I didn't ask that question. "I'm excited to be going with you guys, too."

Pulling the door open, he extended one arm. "After you."

His broad, hard chest took up most of the doorway, and my shoulder brushed against him as I squeezed through the tight space. Quickening my step, I barely squeaked out a quick, "Lock it, please," as I handed him my keys. My body went super hot, and my brain went a little soft as the brief contact affected me in a way that didn't happen often.

A black Mercedes was parked behind my Toyota in the driveway. At the passenger door stood Eli, holding the car door open for me. "Here ya go, Rebel."

"You two don't have to dote on me, you know." I slipped into the seat. "But I have to admit that I love it. You're both such perfect gentlemen."

"Thanks," Eli said as he closed the door then got into the back-seat. "We're trying to be."

Harman got in behind the steering wheel and looked back at his son. "Seatbelt."

"Oh, yeah." Eli buckled himself in. "I don't know why I always forget about that."

Harman watched Eli putting on his seatbelt through the rearview mirror. "Me, neither. You've had to wear one forever." He turned his head to look at me. "So, what's your favorite pizza?"

"Pepperoni." I knew I was boring, but I didn't like experimenting with all the latest pizza trends.

"Mine, too." Harman wiggled his eyebrows. "Great minds think alike."

"I like cheese pizza," Eli informed me. "Me and Mom like cheese. Dad likes pepperoni, and now you do, too."

"It's nice to have someone on my side for a change," Harman said as he pulled out of my driveway.

A Rolls Royce slowly drove past us. The driver's nose was firmly in the air and the back windows were tinted so darkly you couldn't see a thing inside. "Look! It's Mrs. Snotgrass."

"Snodgrass," Harman corrected him. "She's the head of the HOA. Her family comes from ancient money, so I've heard. She only stays here a few months out of the year, and that's when we have monthly meetings. The rest of the year we're free."

"Since she's here and it's the first of November, am I in for my first meeting?" I asked, feeling a little uneasy about having to go to a meeting already, especially with me being the only person in the neighborhood who wasn't dripping in money.

"I'm sure you will." Harman sensed my uneasiness. "And don't worry—you'll have me there with you."

"It's certainly nice to have a friend to go with to something like that." I was having trouble reading Harman, but I had the feeling that he might like me as a little more than just a friend. As handsome and successful as the man was, I had my reservations about that.

He'd been clear about the fact that he would let his ex-wife move back in with him if she ever wanted to. Getting involved romantically with someone in such a precarious situation would be risky. And I had the feeling that I could fall hard for this man if I let myself—one kiss and he would ruin me for other men, I just knew it.

He pulled up at the pizza place and we found the parking lot packed. "Seems we're not the only ones who want to play," I said as I scanned the parking lot for an empty space. "Over there, Harman. That spots empty."

Heading that way, he pulled in, then Eli hauled butt out the door. "Oh, boy!"

We had to hurry to keep up with the lightning-fast kid. I was only a few steps behind Eli when we got to the door, but Harman managed to reach over my shoulder and grab the door before I could. The front of his entire body pressed against the back of mine, and I nearly dropped into a melty puddle on the floor as heat washed over me once again.

Walking into the place, which was filled with noisy people and machines, I could barely hear a thing Harman said, but I followed Eli. The kid looked like he knew exactly where he was going. Through the crowds we went until I saw a doorway. Eli walked through it and into an area that was about thirty times quieter. "Wow, this place is pure chaos." Eli pulled out a chair for me at a table for four and I sat. "Thank you, kind sir."

Eli giggled. "My pleasure, kind lady."

Harman's gentle smile seemed fixed to his face as he sat across from me. "I'm used to all the racket. I guess having a kid for eight years will make you immune to the noise."

"That must be it," I said with a smile as I picked up the menu from the little metal stand in the middle of the table.

"I'll try not to be too loud," Eli remarked.

Looking at him, my heart melted a little. I didn't want him to change a thing for me. "Don't you dare, Eli. I love you just the way you are, noise and all."

Stronger women than I would have cracked at his crooked grin—the kid was just too sweet. "I love you just the way you are, too, Rebel."

Harman's eyes glittered with affection as he looked at his son. "That's really sweet."

I ran my hand through Eli's shaggy locks. "How about you let me trim your hair when we get done here? I found my scissors. And I took some classes in college, so I do know what I'm doing. I won't scalp you or anything like that."

"Can she, Dad?" he asked with pleading eyes.

Harman nodded. "Sounds good to me." Then he ran his hand through his own sandy locks. "Can you trim me up, too, Rebel?"

The thought of being that close to the man for that long—and getting to run my fingers through his thick strands—made my insides quiver. "Uh huh."

"Cool." Harman picked up a menu. "Care to share a pitcher of beer with me, Rebel?"

"Sure." I wasn't much of a beer drinker, but it wouldn't hurt to have some with him.

Turning the menu over, Harman's eyes went wide. "Oh, wait. They've got a full bar here. I had no idea. It must be hidden away in the back somewhere. How about a Jack and Coke instead?"

"Sounds even better." Perusing the food on the menu, I saw the pizzas came in a few different styles. "Can we get our pepperoni in the deep dish-style?"

"Is there any other way?" Harman asked with a grin.

"Dad always gets it that way," Eli told me. "Me and Mom like the thin crust. Can I go play while you guys wait for the food? You can call me on my phone when I need to come back to eat. I saw Jason and David from my class out there and want to play with them."

"Get after it." Harman handed him some money. "Go to the front and buy one of those wristbands that let you have unlimited playtime."

Swiping the cash, Eli sped away like his legs were on fire. "Man, that boy can run, can't he?" I turned my head as the waiter came up on the other side of me.

Harman ordered the food and drinks, then put his elbows on the table, steepling his fingers and looking at me. "I've been wondering something about you, Rebel."

I'd been wondering lots of things about him. "Is that so?"

"Yeah." He licked his lips. "I've been wondering if you're seeing anyone."

Oh, shit!

"Um, no. Not for some time. I've been out of the dating loop for a while, what with my work schedule and buying the house and all that." There'd been one intern who'd had the hots for me, but that didn't pan out. And I didn't really want Harman to know about that, for some reason. "Why do you ask?" I had my fingers crossed underneath the table, hoping he'd give me a good response—even though I knew dating him was risky.

Leaning back in his chair, he nodded at the waiter who delivered our drinks. "Thanks." Waiting for the man to leave us, he continued, "It's just that you're an amazing woman, and I can't understand how you haven't been scooped up yet."

Not quite what I was looking for. I wondered if I'd been picking up on the wrong signals from him. "I haven't been available to be scooped, I suppose. I've slowed down recently at work, but up until a couple months back, I tended to spend around twelve to fifteen hours a day at the clinic."

"Now that you've got your own home to take care of, you've decided to spend more time at home than at work, huh?" He took a drink, peering at me over the rim of the short glass.

"That's exactly it. The minute I knew I'd be getting my own home and getting out of that apartment, I knew I'd find myself wanting to spend more time at home." I couldn't wait to start bringing animals home with me and helping to rehabilitate them there. "I'll most likely find an animal or two to bring home tomorrow while I'm at work."

"Eli will be pleased." Harman sat his glass down. "It's nice that you get to work with animals when you like them so much. I had a dog when I was a kid, but other than that I haven't had any pets. And Tara said she's allergic to pet dander, so we never had any pets after we got married. Eli should be able to at least play with them, now that she's not around."

And there it was—that sad look again. "Hey, what do you say we don't bring her up for the rest of the night? Your mood shifts whenever you start thinking about her. And we've got lots of other things we can talk about—she's not the only woman on the planet, after all."

The slightest smile curved his lips. "You're right. She's not." And the twinkle in his eyes made moisture blossom between my thighs.

7

HARMAN

REBEL'S sweet scent lingered about me even after we'd left her at her home. Her body had been so close to mine as she'd trimmed my hair that the vanilla-based perfume she wore still hung in my nostrils.

I'd invited her to our nightly swim, but she claimed exhaustion from all the unpacking she'd done that weekend. Even exhausted, the woman glowed. I wondered if she could ever look bad. I had the feeling she was one of those people who simply woke up looking great.

"Dad, can I take the night off of swimming, too, like Rebel?" Eli asked as we walked into our home. "I'm 'sausted, too."

"Sure, Little Buddy. Just pop into the shower real quick, then get into bed. I'll come tuck you in, and I'll do my laps afterward." With all that pizza to work off, I didn't want to miss my nightly therapy and exercise.

Later, as I swam lap after lap in the pool, I lost myself in fantasies of Rebel. I could practically feel her long legs wrapped around my waist, her silky hair moving between my fingers. Her body pressed against mine.

Our lips met, and explosions went off inside my head. Blinking, I came out of my little fantasy. I had no idea if Rebel would be interested in dating me. I'd probably blown my chances the moment I told her I would take Tara back, even if just for Eli's sake. That should've scared her off.

The thing was, I didn't know why I told her that. It wasn't a lie, but it wasn't like Tara had ever hinted at coming back. My ex was off doing whatever she wanted without a thought for me or Eli, and there I was, building a wall around myself and using the idea that she might come back as mortar for the rocks.

Rebel didn't strike me as fool, and it would be foolish to get involved with a man who'd told her something like that. The truth was, I had no desire to get back together with Tara—our relationship had never been easy. But I knew I wanted her in our son's life, and I would do anything to get that to happen again.

A boy needs his mother. Mine had been a significant influence on me. Not that Tara was a very good influence, but she *was* Eli's mother, and she should be in his life.

I had the feeling Eli would be running to Rebel's as soon as he saw her driving up each day. He'd be spending time with her, not his mother. And that would be okay, but it wasn't the same as having his mother around.

My head a mess, I ended my swim session earlier than usual then headed up to my room to shower. As the hot water ran over my tired body, I leaned back on the warm, tiled walls.

Rebel's laughter filled my head. She and I had played skee-ball at the pizza place. She wasn't very good at it, and I'd moved in behind her, taking her hand and helping her toss the ball to hit the main hole. She'd missed all her other throws, and I'd wanted to help her out. I hadn't done it just for the sake of getting so close to her.

Or had I?

All throughout the night, I kept managing to get her body to graze mine. I hadn't actually planned these bits of contact, but maybe my subconscious had me making sure we touched as often as possible.

The thing was, each touch seemed better than the last; even the slightest graze sent the best sensations through me. No one had ever affected me that way. I thought it was either a sign that we'd have fantastic chemistry or that we'd have too much passion between us to sustain a healthy relationship.

I knew hot sex didn't equal a long-term relationship. In my experience, it almost made things more difficult. Once the heat faded away with time, all you'd be left with is the bland, everyday life of most married couples. Sometimes when the passion fades, you realize you have nothing in common with the other person at all.

But I'd seen exceptions to that in my life—though not from my parents. Those two seemed more like brother and sister in my mind. They got along okay, but there was no touching or any signs of lingering love or desire for one another.

Maybe I'd had poor role models in the relationship area. Perhaps that's why I'd married a woman I didn't love and thought that marriage was nothing more than a union between two people to make a family.

It had hurt when Tara left. Not because I'd miss her. Not because I loved her, but because she'd walked away from what I thought would be our forever. I thought that we were building a life and a family together.

I don't know why I thought that. She'd made it clear that we'd never have any more children. We'd had one argument over that when Eli was three. I thought he should have a sibling, but Tara thought that she never wanted to have another baby.

But maybe she just didn't want to have another one with me. She certainly seemed to be having more sex now than she'd ever had with me. In two years, she'd gone through seven men. The last three years of our marriage, we'd had sex maybe once a month, if that.

And what bothered me the most was that I was okay with that. I'd accepted that as the reality of my marriage. So when Tara had decided that it wasn't enough for her, it had hurt. It hurt because she'd come to terms with our lack of love and decided it wasn't okay. And I'd come to terms with it and decided it was tolerable.

So tolerable that I'd tell a woman I was attracted to that I'd let the mother of my son back into my home and my life even though I'd never been happy with that life.

What a moron!

Tara might have a lot of faults, but she'd been right about one thing—our marriage had needed to end.

Getting out of the shower, I toweled off, then went to put on my pajamas before getting into my king-sized bed—a bed I'd only briefly shared with my wife. A bed we'd had sex in only once before she told me she couldn't live with me anymore.

"Tomorrow, I'm getting a new bed." I rolled over and turned off the lamp on the nightstand. "I've got to make some changes, or I'll never be truly happy."

Rebel's words from earlier that evening rang in my ears: "*Your mood shifts whenever you start thinking about her...she's not the only woman on the planet, after all.*"

Rebel must've seen something in my eyes or demeanor that I hadn't noticed before. And it was time to change that. Thinking about Tara wasn't helping me at all. Feeling sorry for our son wasn't changing a thing.

I'd said everything imaginable to Tara to get her to realize how important she was to our son, but nothing had made a difference. She'd found her freedom after seven years of being married to me, and she wasn't looking back at either of us.

Maybe it was time for me to experience some freedom of my own —freedom from the guilt of my failed marriage. Freedom from Tara's irresponsibility.

Lying in bed, looking up at the ceiling, I knew I had to move on. For Eli's sake just as much as mine. I had to stop trying to get his mother to be someone she wasn't.

But even as I thought that, my heart ached for Eli: my poor little boy whose mother had run so fast to get away from me that she'd left him behind, too.

Why had I never tried to get her to fall in love with me? Why had I never tried to find something to love in her? Why had I rushed into marriage when we could've gone about being Eli's parents separately?

Back then I'd wanted a normal family, no matter what. From the moment we got the DNA results back a week after she'd found me,

I'd told Tara what we'd do. We'd get married, and I'd move my room-mate out of my apartment, so she could move in.

Being young and easily influenced by her parents, who didn't want the responsibility of taking on the baby or the expenses of the pregnancy and delivery, Tara had done what we'd all told her to do. So, in a tiny church that her grandmother was a member of, we got married just one month after she'd hunted me down and told me the news.

Our first night together hadn't been special at all. She couldn't drink, but I'd had a few beers to help settle my nerves. There wasn't money for a real honeymoon. We'd gone to my apartment—her new home—and eaten some frozen pizza.

That night hadn't been anything like our first encounter in the bathroom, either. That had been rushed and wild—fun, even. But the night of our wedding, with both of us feeling reluctant, both of us unsure about whether we'd done the right thing, we'd gotten into bed and awkwardly kissed. We closed our eyes and pretended there wasn't anything wrong with what we were doing. And we'd had sex.

I'd never made love to anyone in my life. But as I lay in my king-sized bed—a bed I'd once shared with my wife—I knew that if Rebel and I ever had the opportunity to do anything so intimate, we'd be making love, not just having sex. And the truth was that scared me.

Why could I see myself falling in love with a woman I'd only spent time with twice? Was something wrong with me? Was I grasping at straws?

Knowing that Tara was out there having the time of her life without her son or me might've been affecting me in ways I hadn't realized. It made no sense why I'd be thinking so much about a woman I'd barely met. And yet I couldn't stop thinking about Rebel.

In my present state, I felt if I did make a move on Rebel, I might end up drowning her with how hard I'd hold onto her. As it was, I had a hard time dragging myself away from her each time I had to leave her at her door.

My lips had itched to kiss hers both nights I'd walked her to her door. My stomach had twisted itself in knots as I walked away from her each time. I'd had to clench my fists at my sides and force my reluctant feet to take me away from her.

How had Rebel Saxe done so much to me so quickly, without even trying? And how had she gotten my son to say he loved her already?

"Maybe she's a witch," I smiled as I said the words out loud. "A witch who will steal your heart and then your soul, Harman Hunter. And maybe that of your young son's, too. You should be careful."

But could I? Could I continue to stifle the attraction I felt so completely for her?

What choice did I have?

I'd told her too much about my messy divorce. Worse, I'd made it clear I'd take my ex back if she ever wanted. I'd screwed it all up before I even had a chance in hell with the woman.

It didn't matter that we liked the same mixed drink, the same pizza, or that we'd chosen similar careers. It didn't matter that we could've made the perfect couple. I'd already blown it—I didn't have a shot with the woman.

8

REBEL

AFTER ONLY ONE week had passed, Eli had already proven himself to be the most responsible little boy I'd ever known. Every day he cleaned the cages of a couple of very messy rabbits, making sure they had fresh water, and even bringing lettuce for them each day, too.

At the end of the week, Harman came over to check on how things were going. "So, is Eli working out for you, Rebel?"

"Better than expected." I patted Eli on the back as he put the leash on a Chihuahua who needed some rehabilitating after hip replacement surgery. His owner was a little old lady who couldn't walk him, since she herself had to use a wheelchair to get around.

Eli beamed at me. "I love it, Rebel. I love every single one of these little guys. And I love that you let me do this."

I pulled a twenty dollar bill out of my pocket. "And here's your first week's pay."

Harman cleared his throat as Eli took the money and put it in his own pocket. "You want me to hold that for you, so you don't lose it?"

"Well, here's the thing, Dad." Eli had already told me what he planned on doing with the money, but I didn't know if a single week of work was enough time to prove to his dad that he was ready. It seemed Eli thought it was. "You see, I'd like to spend this money on something. But I need your permission to do it."

Harman looked at me. "I've got a feeling I know what he's going to ask. Before he does, can I ask you something?"

Nodding, I said, "Sure."

"Do you think he's ready?" He eyed me very seriously, and I realized my answer would likely be the deciding factor in whether the kid got what he wanted.

I wanted to be honest with them both. "I've got to say that Eli has surpassed my expectations by miles, Harman. And I'm not just saying that. He listens intently. He follows directions to the T. He doesn't talk back about anything. But most impressive is that he's full of great ideas. And he's Googled information about each animal I've brought home. He's done that all on his own. So, I think—yes. I think he's ready."

Turning his attention back to his son, Harman gave him the go ahead to ask his question. "Shoot, Little Buddy. And I want you to know that I'm extremely proud of you."

The kid glowed as he nodded. "Thanks, you guys. Dad, I'd like to have a dog. That's what I wanna spend my money on. I know he'll need food and a collar and a leash and stuff like that. I could buy him whatever he needs since I have a job now. And I want to pick one out from the animal shelter, too."

We both looked at Harman for his answer, and I crossed my fingers behind my back, hoping he'd approve. "Well, how can I say no when you've proven yourself to be such a capable animal caretaker?"

Eli pumped his fist. "Yes! Can we go tomorrow to look for one?"

Harman looked at me. "Can you make it tomorrow, Rebel?"

"Oh, you want me to come along too?" The thought of spending some more time with him made my heart sing.

"I won't do it without you," he let me know. "You're the expert here, after all."

Eli's eyes bore into me. "Please, Rebel."

"You know I can't say no to that voice." The kid already knew his secret power over me. "Of course, I'll join you guys to help pick out just the right dog for you, Eli."

"I'll be here to pick you up around nine in the morning then," Harman informed me. "We'll go eat some breakfast first then start the search for Eli's first dog."

"Sounds good to me." I couldn't stop smiling after that. Spending the morning with Harman would be a great way to start the weekend.

Getting up bright and early the next day, I braided my hair and put on some warm clothes as a cold front had drifted in during the night. When a knock sounded at my door at precisely nine, I opened it to find Harman standing there. "You could've just honked." I walked out, and he followed behind me.

"Never. That's not what a gentleman does, Rebel." He stepped around me to open the car door for me.

His actions made me smile as I slid into the car. "Thank you, Harman. Morning, Eli. You look pretty happy this morning."

"I am!" He pumped his fist in the air. "I'm getting smiley face pancakes, then a dog! It can't get any better than this!"

Harman got in, grinning from ear to ear. "He's been on cloud nine since last night."

"Yeah," Eli said. "Mom wasn't happy about it, though. She said I can't take it to her house when I go over. But Dad said he doesn't mind taking care of him when that happens. It's not like it happens a lot anyway."

I caught Harman's jaw tightening. "Yeah, well, you'll be going over there next weekend."

"We'll see." Even Eli knew it was a long shot that his mother would pick him up for the weekend.

I decided to change the subject, since just the mention of the woman had wiped the smiles from their faces. "So, smiley face pancakes for you, huh? I'm thinking about some coffee and scrambled eggs, bacon, and hash browns, myself."

Harman cut his eyes at me as he drove ahead. "Where we're going, that plate is called the American Deluxe."

Eli laughed. "That's what Dad always gets when we go to his

favorite café."

"So, another meal we both like." I'd thought it kind of odd that we liked so many of the same things—I figured I'd see just how far our similarities went. "My favorite color is red. Any chance that's yours, too?"

"Mine's blue." He stopped at a red light and looked at me. "So we do have some differences then, don't we?"

"Seems so." I batted my lashes at him. "My eyes are your favorite color, Harman," I teased.

"Yes, they are." He turned his head to the road as the light changed, and I felt a blush heat my cheeks.

Changing the subject again, I asked, "So, how do you like this cold weather we're having?"

"I like it," Eli chimed in. "It's starting to feel like the holidays now. I get out of school early next week because of Thanksgiving. And I get two whole weeks out for Christmas. I can't wait! And I'm gonna have my dog to play with, too. It's gonna be like a dream come true."

"Are you going to be okay with him keeping the dog inside if it gets too cold, Harman?" I asked. "Because I can keep him inside mine if you don't want to."

"I'll let him stay inside if it's cold out. Eli will just have to make sure he's clean and has no fleas." Harman looked at me. "I did have a dog when I was a kid. I know how to care for them, too."

"Good." It was a habit of mine; always making sure people knew how to take care of their pets.

After breakfast, we hit our first shelter. It was a no-kill shelter, and it was clean and well-maintained. It was clear that the people in charge were very thorough with the care of the animals.

Liza, the manager, led us around the place. "And this one here is Doolittle. He's a mini-Yorkie and he came to us from the home of an elderly woman who passed on. We've had him for two weeks, now. He's a little on the nippy side, but we've been working with him to stop that."

"He looks like a girl's dog," Eli remarked as he shook his head. "He's not the one for me."

Liza looked a little miffed but moved on to the next kennel. "This is Roger. He's a mixed breed—we're thinking Doberman and Pitbull. He looks mean, but he's a real sweetie."

"And how did he end up here?" I asked, knowing both breeds to be aggressive if not properly trained.

Liza didn't look directly at me as she said, "His owner was a single woman who decided she didn't want such a large dog anymore."

I looked at Eli. "What do you think, Eli?"

"I think he looks sort of mean, and I don't want him." Eli looked at Liza. "I think I'd like a medium-sized dog or maybe a large one if he's kind of cute and cuddly. Nothing really little. I want to be able to run and play with him. Or I want to be able to hang around with him and just chill sometimes, you know?"

Harman and I laughed at Eli's specificity—the boy had clearly put a lot of thought into this. Liza looked at us as if we were crazy. "I only have what we have here. Maybe you'd like to just walk around and see if any of the dogs meet your qualifications?"

"Sure." Eli broke away from us to walk around. He pointed at a Cocker Spaniel who barked at him as he approached his cage. "No to this one." A mutt wagged its tail at him as he walked toward it, but then started growling as he got closer. "No to you, too, Mr. Growly." One by one, he turned them all down.

So we got back into the car and headed to the next place. "Now this one is going to be a lot rougher than the last one," I let them know. "It's the city pound. They're not as snooty as the other people were, but the dogs might not be in the best of condition, either."

Eli proved just how much research he'd likely done before we came on this outing. "So they kill these dogs if no one takes them after a while, right?"

Nodding, I felt it wouldn't do him any good to lie to him. "Yes. But I still don't want you to pick one just because of that. It's important to make sure that the dog you choose is compatible with your lifestyle."

"I got it, Rebel." Eli didn't seem like he'd try to save them all, but one never knew when faced with such a terrible choice.

"Okay. That said, I'm a real softie and will need you guys to help keep me from taking home every animal on death row." I reached over to pat Harman on the shoulder. "Don't let me fall in love, Harman. Promise me."

He looked at me out of the corner of his eyes. "It might not be that easy, Rebel."

"Distract me if you have to." I was only half-joking. I did have a real problem. "Anything it takes to stop me from looking into their sad eyes, do it."

"You got it," he assured me.

Once we got inside, I had to keep burying my face in Harman's shoulder, so I wouldn't fall in love with every one of the poor dogs we passed. And luckily, it didn't take long for Eli to find his doggy soulmate. "This is him. This is the one."

We left there with a shaggy older Sheepdog who would need tons of grooming. But both he and Eli sat happily in the backseat of the car together. "You two look great together, but I can't wait to give Moppy a makeover once we get to my place."

Nothing could've removed the smile from Eli's face. "How can I love him so much already?"

I thought the same thing about him. "When you know, *you know*." I looked at Harman and tried to fight off a blush, wishing things could be different.

If I didn't fear that he'd take his ex-wife back in a second if it came to that, then I would've been more open with him about the way I felt. But she was always there, lurking in the background of everything we'd done together so far.

Harman pulled into my drive then looked at me. "Hey, after we get the dog cleaned up, want to come to our place? I can get Rene to make whatever you want for dinner. We want to thank you for your help today."

Seemed I'd be spending the entire day and part of the night with this man who I was finding it harder and harder to hide my feelings from. "Sure, that would be nice. And you guys are very welcome. I loved helping you pick out the newest member of your family." And I loved spending time with them, too.

9

HARMAN

"Come on, Rebel, please," Eli begged, trying to convince our neighbor to stay and swim with us.

"I didn't bring my bathing suit, Eli." Rebel ducked her head a bit shyly and fiddled with the front of her shirt, making me think she wasn't feeling too secure about her body—and that possibility blew my mind.

Without realizing what I was doing, words flew out of my mouth before I could catch them. "You have nothing to be shy about, Rebel. Your body's perfect."

"Yeah," Eli chimed in.

Now Rebel's checks blazed red. "You guys, stop. It's not that. It's just that I didn't get my bathing suit, and I don't want to go all the way home and back. That's it, nothing else."

I figured we'd asked her enough times to join our swimming dates with no success that maybe we should give it a rest for a while. "Okay, she's given her answer, Eli."

Cocking her head to one side, Rebel checked the time on her cell, then looked at me. "I've gotta get going. Dinner was great, and I can see Moppy has settled in already. I'll see you guys later."

She began walking out of the pool room, but I wasn't having any of that. "Hey, you can't walk home. First of all, it's cold outside."

Eli wasn't having it either. "And it's dark."

"I'll drive you." I turned to look at Eli. "Nancy is still here. You get changed into your swimming trunks, but don't get into the pool until I get back. I'll let the maid go home after that."

"It's not that cold, Harman," Rebel tried to put me off.

"Yes, it is. And Eli's right, it's dark out, and I can't have you strolling away from my home all alone on a cold, dark night." I hooked my arm through hers as she stood there with her hands on her hips. "What would the neighbors think if I did something as ungentlemanly as that?"

"Night, Eli," she called out as I led her away.

"Night, Rebel," he shouted back at her. "Have sweet dreams."

Out to the garage we went, and I helped her into my favorite sports car: my blue Lambo. "See, I told you my favorite color was blue."

Her eyes sparkled as she looked at the futuristic interior. "You think you can give me a ride around the block before you take me home?"

"I think I can do that." I got in and we sped off, wheels screaming down the drive. "Hold on."

Her hands were on the ceiling, her mouth wide open, and a look of pure joy filled her face. "Oh, shit!"

Sliding around the corner, I gunned it through the straightaway then slammed on the brakes before hitting the actual street. "Sometimes I take this to the track to really let loose." I looked at her. "You should come with me sometime. Maybe next Saturday? If Eli's mother picks him up."

"Just you and me, huh?" she asked with a smile. "That kind of sounds like a date."

I shook my head then took off again, heading down the street at a moderate speed. "*That's* not a date. Adding in dinner and maybe some dancing? Now that's a date," I teased.

She tossed her head to one side. "Throw in a box of chocolates, and you've got yourself a date for Saturday night, Harman."

I don't know what response I'd been expecting from my teasing, but it hadn't been that. I slowed to a stop at the end of the street. "You would really go out on a real date with me?"

A sly grin moved over her ruby red lips. "Like I said, throw in a box of chocolates, Harman."

I just sat there, staring at her. "You're too good for me. You should know that right off the bat."

"You think you're worse off than you really are," she rallied back. "You just need a little more excitement in your life."

My brain was throwing out all sorts of reasons why a woman like Rebel shouldn't give a guy like me—a single dad with one failed marriage under his belt—a chance. But my heart told it to shut the hell up. Right now, the girl wanted me. Right now, she was willing to take that risk. And I found that exciting.

"Your mother named you aptly, Rebel." I sped off again, taking the next right and making her squeal with joy.

"So is that a yes, Harman?" she asked as she held on tight.

"I thought *I* was the one asking *you* out, not the other way around." I turned another corner, making the tires smoke. "So, is it a yes, Rebel?"

"If you don't kill me on this ride home, I'll be happy to go out with you next Saturday night." She gasped as I hit the gas hard and heavy, taking the last stretch as fast as I could before coming to a stop in front of her drive.

"Here we are—safe and sound." I eased the car into the driveway, parking behind her little car.

Getting out of the car, I met her in front of it, then walked with her to the door. Waiting for her to unlock it, I leaned one hand on the doorframe. "I've gotten the site set up for the scholarship. I decided to include doctors of all kinds, Rebel. You should join the contest, too. Who knows, you might be one of the two hundred winners I choose next month. I'll make the selections on Christmas Eve. It's kind of like giving two hundred people one hell of a Christmas gift."

"Impressive." She leaned her shoulder on the other side of the door. "I've been wondering why it took you until yesterday to visit me. I guess you were busy with the website?"

"You missed me?" I asked with what I hoped was a sexy grin. It felt like it'd been ages since I'd even tried to flirt with a woman, and I was feeling a little out of sorts.

She nodded. "But now that I know why you were so busy I suppose I can forgive you for making me wait so long to see that handsome face of yours."

"Then you'll have to forgive me in advance for this coming week, I'm afraid. My parents are coming to stay with Eli starting tomorrow." I hadn't even told him about that yet. I wanted it to be a surprise—he loved spending time with his Nana and Papa.

"And why's that?" She twirled a tendril of hair that had fallen loose from the braid she wore.

Another strand hung limply on the other side of her face, and I reached out to twirl it around my own finger. "Because I've got to get on a plane tomorrow morning. I'm heading to Los Angeles for a convention that lasts until Friday."

"Then you'll be back on Friday?" She looked at me with shining eyes. "And you'll stop by, right?"

"After I check on things at the hospital, I will." I moved my hand away from her face. The urge to kiss her was driving me mad. But I wanted that kiss to mean something. I wanted it to be special—something we'd remember forever.

I wanted everything we did to be memorable. I didn't want to make the same mistakes I'd made before. This time, I wanted to feel it all, not just go through the motions.

Taking out her cell, she ran her finger over the screen then handed it to me. "Put your number in for me. I might want to hear your voice while you're gone."

She really will miss me.

I put my number in. "Call it. I want to have yours, too. Just in case I start to miss the sound of your voice." I'd definitely be calling her— every night, if she'd let me.

When she looked at what I'd written under the name of the contact, she smiled. "So, Hot Guy Next Door, what are you going to put me in as?"

My cell vibrated, and I answered the call, saving the contact. "Guess."

She stood there watching me type it in then took a guess, "Blue Eyes."

"Close." I turned the phone so that she could see it. "Possible Woman of my Dreams."

"Possible?" She laughed. "Oh, I am definitely the woman of your dreams."

Again, the urge to kiss her nearly overwhelmed me. I settled for running the back of my fingers along her cheek, feeling her soft skin and trying to memorize every line of her beautiful face. "I've gotta get back to Eli. I don't want him getting into the pool without me. He can swim like a fish, but I've had one too many kids show up in the ER who knew how to swim but drowned anyway."

"Oh, God!" She stood up straight. "Go. Hurry. You've put a terrible image in my head now. Hurry."

I turned to leave, but I looked over my shoulder before she closed the door. "Night, Rebel."

"I had a great time." She kissed her palm then blew it at me. "See you on Friday, then. 'Night."

She closed the door and I floated back to my car. It was a new sensation unlike any I'd ever felt. I felt light, like I could fly if I only raised my arms and lifted my feet off the ground.

The drive back home went a little too fast. I was still in a daze when I got back and went to the pool room and saw Eli sitting at the edge of the pool, his feet in the water. "What took ya so long?" He jumped in, making a big splash.

"Swim your behind over to the steps." I still had to change. "You know better than that."

He swam over to them then sat there, waiting as I walked to the dressing room. "Why do you look like that?"

"Like what?" I started unbuttoning my shirt as I walked along slowly.

"Like you just woke up and had a really good dream." He splashed water at me as I walked by him.

"Never mind." I went into the dressing room and stopped in front of the mirror. *You do look like you've just woken up. What has she woken inside of you that's been asleep your whole life, Harman Hunter?*

Whatever it was, I didn't want it to ever go away. I wanted it to keep waking and waking until it was fully alive and with me all the time.

I'd seen men with a skip in their step and smiles on their faces before. I never understood where all that inner joy could come from. But now I got it.

It's like every person is only half alive before we meet that perfect partner for us. We don't allow ourselves to believe it could really be true, that there has always been a person out there who could bring out such wonderful feelings in us. Feelings that were always there, but hidden so far back that we were never aware of them in the least.

Rebel had sparked something in me that had brought me fully awake. I knew it was only a smolder so far, but soon—after we kissed, held hands, nuzzled each other—it would grow into a flame. And then, after we made love, it would turn into a blazing inferno. I knew it would.

What we had was undeniable, and it was already too late to stop it from becoming a fire that no one could ever put out.

10

REBEL

GETTING Harman's number was the best decision I'd made in a very long time. The nightly calls we shared were out of this world amazing!

I found out so much about Harman that week, each of us telling each other every detail about our lives. He called me each night when he got back to the hotel after the day's classes and lectures.

Equally as important that week, I'd met his parents when they'd accompanied Eli to my place the first day they were there. I'd even eaten dinner with them a couple of times.

Ida and Richard were as nice as any two people could be; it was no surprise they'd raised such an amazing son. And when I told Harman about them inviting me to dinner that first night, he said that they must like me already because they never had much to say to his ex. I took that as a great sign.

The week went by slowly, and when Friday came around, I was readier than ever to see the man I'd gotten so close to. He'd made it back to town but was at the hospital checking on things as I headed home from work.

I'd just pulled into my drive and gotten in the house when Eli came walking in my backdoor, looking sad. "She's not coming."

No!

I went to grab him a cookie and a bottle of water. "Have a seat, Slugger. What do you mean, she's not coming? I talked to your father last night and he said she was definitely coming to get you today and would be bringing you back on Sunday. He said she'd even mentioned something about taking you to her family's for Thanksgiving." I was hoping Eli had just misunderstood her.

He didn't even take a bite of the cookie as he sat down, his head drooping. "She just called me. She told me she's got to go out of town on business. It just came up."

I took him by the chin, lifting his face so I could get a good look at him. "You've been crying." He had little lines down his cheeks that told me as much. "Eli, try not to cry. I'm sure it's something super important that she just couldn't get out of."

His cell rang and he took it out of his pocket. "It's her. Maybe she changed her mind." A smile broke out over his lips as he answered the phone with excitement. "Mom? Did you get out of it?"

I could just make out her tense voice as she said, "No, baby. But you were crying and had hung up on me, and it made me worry about you. I don't want you to think I don't love you. Why would you say that to me?"

I sat there, trying not to roll my eyes at the woman's question. She hadn't seen him in a month now. What did she expect him to think?

"You're not coming to get me?" he asked, instead of answering her question. "I don't want to talk to you."

Before he ended the call, I held out my hand. "Can I talk to her, Eli?" The rational part of me knew that I had no business butting in here, but Eli had quickly nestled his way into my heart, and I was tired of seeing him hurt.

Eli pushed the phone across the table without saying a word. I picked it up and tried to sound nonjudgmental, but it wasn't easy. "Hi, this is Rebel, Eli's neighbor. Your son is helping me with my animals; I'm a vet and he's been such a great help to me. He's really got a knack with animals."

"He talks about you every day," she said with a hint of reluctance in her nasally voice. I walked away a bit from Eli as I listened to his mother, not wanting him to hear every part of our conversation. "I'm glad he has such a good time with the animals."

"Yeah." I didn't know how to go about things with the woman. And I knew Harman wouldn't want me telling her anything personal. "Um, Eli's really upset, Tara. May I call you that? Eli told me your name. He talks about you every day, too." That wasn't a lie. He'd told me how much he missed her every single day.

"Yeah, you can call me that." I heard her sighing. "So he talks about me all the time?"

Maybe not all the time, but he talked about her enough. "He does. And he misses you so much. I'm sure you're busy running your business, and I try to tell him that's the only reason he doesn't get to see you. But when can you make some time to see him?" I'd never even asked if she lived in Seattle. Maybe the distance was too far to make it feasible for her to come get him. "Where is it that you live, anyway? He's never told me."

"In Seattle," she said. I tried to hold back any sound trying to emerge from my throat, but I wanted to hiss at the woman. I really didn't understand why she hadn't seen her kid in a month when she lived in the same damn city. "I've opened this boutique and it's taking more time than I thought it would. I want to sell it and try something else, but my ex doesn't want to help me."

Good for Harman!

"I'm sure your business does take up a lot of your time, but there's got to be time after you close. When does your shop close?" Maybe if I asked the right questions she'd see just how easy it would be to fit her son into her life.

"Six," came her answer, and I tried not to snort.

"That's pretty early." I shouldn't have had to tell her that, but it seemed she needed to hear it. "That leaves a fair amount of time for you to pick Eli up and take him to dinner. He'd love that. I bet his father would even bring him to meet you anywhere you wanted. I bet he'd even wait around and bring him back home after you and Eli were done."

"Yeah, I've heard how much time you've been spending with my ex," her tone was sharp. "I hope you're not after his money."

"I'm not after anything," I replied sternly. I was not about to let this woman lecture me. "I care about your son. I love this kid. And I'd like to see him happy. Every time you let your plans fall through, it tears this little man apart, and I think you should know that. I'm not your ex. I'm not trying to hurt you by telling you lies. Eli loves you, Tara. He misses you terribly. Do you know that it's been a month since you've last seen your son?"

"It hasn't been that long." She went quiet for a second or two. "Has it?"

"It has." I paused, letting that sink in. "I know because he counts the days."

"I really am out of town. I had to fly to Los Angeles to pick up items for the boutique here. It's easier to make selections when I can feel the textures." She paused then added, "I'm not lying."

"I never assumed you were." I didn't want the call to end without her making some firm plans to see her son. "What's next weekend looking like for you?"

"I don't know if Harman will let me have him if it's not my turn." I found it hard to believe she'd even think such a thing.

"I think he might." I walked back to Eli and ran my head over the top of his head as he laid it on the table, looking miserable. "If Harman will let you have him next weekend, I'm sure Eli would love to spend some time with you. That's a great suggestion—even it's only for one night." I tried to make it sound like it'd been Tara's idea; Eli didn't need to hear me trying to convince his mother to spend time with him. "You're his mother, of course he'll be overjoyed to spend even thirty minutes with you. He only has one mother in this whole world. Don't take that for granted."

She sniffled. "Yeah, I'll get him on Friday when I get back from my family's place in Portland. They just moved, and their place is a wreck right now, otherwise I'd take him with me for Thanksgiving."

"Fair enough." It was better than nothing. "So, he can count on you coming next Friday. What time should I tell him to be ready for?"

"Five," she said with a sigh. "I know you probably don't believe me, but I really have lost track of time. I thought it had only been a week or so since I saw him last. I talk to him every day."

"Yeah, I know. Time can get away from anyone. The thing about time, though, is that you can't get it back once it's gone. Don't let it slip by." I patted Eli on the back. "Your mom will get you in one week, Slugger. How does that sound?"

He lifted his head. "Really?"

"I'll let you tell him, Tara," I said before handing Eli the phone.

He talked excitedly to her about what they could do while she had him, and my heart finally felt a little fuller. It felt a little heavy too, as I worried that she wouldn't come through again. Overall, I felt a lot of hope that she would.

A knock on my front door had my pulse speeding up as I knew it had to be Harman on the other side. I rushed to open it, only to find a stranger. "Um, hello."

He handed me an envelope. "Your presence is required at the HOA meeting on the day before Thanksgiving." And then he turned and started heading toward the next house—Harman's.

"Hey, I can take that for him." I thought I'd save the man the long walk up the driveway. "Harman Hunter's son is right here, and he'll be here soon as well. I can give that to him."

He looked at me for a moment then handed one of the envelopes to me. "I guess that'll be alright. Make sure he gets it. Every home-owner must be present at this meeting."

"He'll get it." I took the other envelope, then closed the door. When I turned around, I saw Eli had gotten off the phone and was glowing. He looked so happy. "It turned out good then?"

"Great!" He wrapped his arms around me, hugging me tightly. "She's sorry, Rebel. She's really sorry. And she's going to make things better. She told me so. And I believe her."

"I do, too." I hugged him back.

He let go of me as the front door opened and his father walked inside. "Dad!" He ran to Harman, who immediately scooped him up.

"Mom's not coming today, but she is coming next Friday, and she promises that things are going to change."

"Great?" Harman looked at me in confusion. "Last I heard she was still coming today."

I shook my head. "She's in Los Angeles."

"Okay." He put Eli down as he looked at me. "Well, Mom and Dad need to get back home."

I nodded. "I know. They've got a funeral to attend in the morning. And the following day there's some kind of reunion for your father's high school class. He said it might be the last one ever."

He nodded his head then look back down at his son. "I'm sorry I have to take you home now, bud." He ran his hand over Eli's head as the boy leaned against him.

"Don't be." I moved forward then put my hand on Eli's shoulder. "Because I thought I might join you two this evening for your swim. We can have cannonball contests in your pool."

Eli's fist shot into the air. "Yes! I'm so gonna beat you guys."

"Thank you," Harman whispered.

"You're welcome," I whispered back.

Sometime or another I would need to tell him what I'd done, but until then I could only hope that I wouldn't be put into the doghouse over it.

11

HARMAN

SITTING at the side of the pool, Rebel and I moved our feet back and forth in the warm water as Eli showed off his diving skills. "And this one's called the pencil." Jumping up as high as he could, he landed in the water with barely any splash at all.

"The pencil, huh?" Rebel mused. "Yeah, I can see that."

Nudging her shoulder with mine, I said quietly, so Eli wouldn't hear, "Maybe you could sneak back over after Eli goes to bed."

Her blue eyes dropped. "I should come clean with you before we get any further into whatever this is between us."

"Come clean?" I had no idea what she was referring to, but I doubted there was anything she could say that would make me take back my invitation.

"Yeah." Looking at me, she chewed her lower lip before going on. "Eli was a real disaster when he got to my house. He told me about his mother cancelling on him again."

"And this one is the backsplash!" Eli shouted. He turned around with his back to the water then fell in, making a horrible slapping sound with his back.

Rebel winced. "Ow." She looked over at Moppy, who was

snoozing on the floor by the door, far enough away that he wouldn't get wet. "Did you see that? Even the dog flinched."

But Eli came up with a grin on his face. "That one always stings." He climbed up the ladder to do another jump. "Now I'll show you guys my dives. I've been practicing them a lot this week."

"That's good to hear, Little Buddy." I hoped he'd be so busy with those that he'd let us finish the conversation Rebel had begun. "We'll watch. You don't have to announce each dive."

"K." Eli walked down the diving board, looking at the water.

I looked back to Rebel, who was chewing her lip again. "You were saying?"

"Um," she mumbled. "Okay. So, my heart was aching for Eli and then his mother called, and I overheard what he said to her."

"What did he say to her?"

"That he thinks she doesn't love him." Rebel's eyes cut to the pool as Eli took another dive. "Great one!" She clapped then looked back at me. "Anyway, he wasn't happy with her at all and was about to hang up on her. I asked if I could talk to her."

"Why?" I didn't think my current love interest needed to be talking to my ex about anything.

"Because I know she hasn't listened to you about Eli." She inched her fingers toward mine, barely touching my fingertips. "It just felt like the right thing to do at the time."

"What did you tell her?" I asked, feeling kind of prickly now. "About us?"

"Nothing about us." She looked away. "But I think she kind of knows we've got something going on; she mentioned that Eli has told her how much time we've spent together. She warned me that I better not to be after your money. I told her I wasn't after anything."

"You're not?" I leaned in, nudging my shoulder against hers. "Nothing at all?" Suddenly Rebel talking to Tara didn't seem so important.

Her grin made my heart skip a beat. "I think *you're* the one who's after *me*. So, it wasn't a complete lie."

Nodding, I agreed. "Yeah, I am after you, Rebel Saxe. And I'm sorry about tonight. We made such big plans and all for nothing. This weekend was going to be about you and me, and now it can't be."

"What's this we're doing now?" she asked, then laid her head on my shoulder. "This is nice. Just being with you is enough for me."

"Yeah?" Well, I wanted a bit more than what would be acceptable in front of my son. "So, you don't feel like you're missing out on those thousands of kisses I've promised you? I better step up my game."

Pulling her head off my shoulder, her eyes met mine. "Talking to you over the phone all week has made me feel closer to you than I've ever felt to anyone. And yes. I am missing those kisses you promised me each night when we ended our calls."

I couldn't wait to get to that part, but we still had a few things that needed discussing. "So, what did you and Tara talk about, then?"

"I just told her how much Eli missed her and how he needed her in his life." Rebel watched Eli as he stepped up on the diving board again. "You're doing great, Eli."

"Thanks," he shouted back before diving off again.

Her eyes came back to me. "She didn't even realize how much time has passed since she's seen him. When I pointed it out, she really seemed taken aback. And afterward, she told Eli things would be different. I hope she meant it."

"Me, too." My hand inched closer until it took hers. I held it hidden between us, so Eli wouldn't see. "On second thought, I don't want you to sneak back over tonight. I don't want it to be cheap like that. I want to spend the entire weekend with you. I want things to be memorable and perfect. The thought that you'd have to get up and leave me before Eli wakes up doesn't sit well with me. You understand, right?"

"I do." She smiled, and it lit me up from the inside out. "I like that you want things to be so special. That's never seemed to matter to anyone else."

"You matter to me more than any woman ever has." I wanted to kiss her so damn badly, it hurt. "I don't want to rush this. But I don't want to wait so long that the fire dies out either."

I'd never done anything like this; I didn't really know what I was doing. But I knew I wanted to build a foundation that would stand the test of time for us. The hours-long conversations we'd had during the week had sent me head-first into infatuation with the woman, and I couldn't wait to make this thing with Rebel real.

Arching one dark brow, she asked, "Do you think that's possible, Harman? That taking our time could extinguish the fire?"

I didn't know for sure. "I don't want to take that chance." I knew that I was capable of living a life without love in it. The only love I'd ever had during my marriage was the love I had for my son. I would've done anything for that kid, but I was ready to experience a different kind of love now, too. And I was sure that Rebel was the right woman to build that with.

Worn out, Eli swam up to the stairs. "I'm getting out. I'm getting tired."

"Time for me to go," Rebel said as she let go of my hand and got up. She'd worn a red one-piece bathing, and as she walked away, she ran her slender fingers along the elastic that made the suit cling to her ass.

Creamy skin, a round ass, hips that begged for my hands to grab hold and pull her close. The image of me grinding my hard cock against her wet mound made my mouth water. I got up, too, putting my hand against the small of her back as she walked in front of me. I heard her sharp intake of breath and loved the reaction my touch had on her.

Eli wrapped a towel around himself. "Hey, tomorrow can we go see that new movie with the wizards and warlocks in it?"

"I think so," I said as we followed him to the door of the pool room. His dog got up, stretching to get ready to follow Eli anywhere.

Rebel hadn't said anything, and Eli stopped to turn around and look at her. "So, can we, Rebel?"

"Oh, me, too?" she asked, seeming surprised.

"Of course, you too." Eli turned back around and continued walking.

"Oh." She looked at me with a smile. "If your dad doesn't mind me tagging along, then I'd loved to go with you guys."

"Dad doesn't mind at all, Rebel." He kept walking without looking back at us. "Don't you notice how much 'tention he pays to you?"

Reaching around, Rebel took my hand off her back, giving me a look that said we were skating on thin ice. "Do you mind, Harman? If I join you tomorrow?"

"I'd mind it if you didn't join us, Rebel." I put my hand right back where it had been. Then leaned in close to whisper, "He can't see what I'm doing."

She didn't say a thing, just looked at me with worried eyes. I didn't understand what she was concerned about.

"Okay, I'm going to take a shower, then get into bed," Eli said. "See you in fifteen minutes when you come to tuck me in, Dad. 'Night, Rebel. I'm glad you finally came swimming with us."

"Me, too." Rebel ran her hand over his head. "See you tomorrow then. Have sweet dreams." She headed toward the dressing room where she'd left her clothes.

I caught up to her. "You seem a little edgy about Eli seeing anything untoward between us."

"I don't want him to see his mother next weekend and tell her that something is going on between us." Rebel stopped just outside the door. "This is their first weekend together in a long time, and I don't want it spoiled by her feeling emotional about you dating me."

I hadn't even thought about that. "I don't think she gives a shit, to be honest with you. It's not like she loved me."

"You know, you've told me that more than once. You two might not have openly expressed love for one another, but there's no way two people can live together for six years and not have love for one another." Her hand went to her hip as she pursed her red lips. "So, don't be shocked if Tara gets a little jealous or hurt when she finds out about us. It would be perfectly natural. Didn't you feel that way when you first found out about her seeing someone else? And don't hide behind your male bravado and lie to me."

"No, I wouldn't say it was jealousy that I felt when I found out about the first guy she dated after leaving me." I paused, thinking of how best to describe what I'd felt back then. "It was more of just an uneasy feeling. And to be perfectly honest, it had a hell of a lot more to do with Eli and the thought that there'd be another man acting as a father figure to him than it had to do with Tara."

"I can see that." Her hand moved off her hip, floating through the air to run through her damp hair. "But I also know what you've told me about letting her come back to live with you if she wanted to."

I winced, regretting for the hundredth time that I'd told her that. Reaching out, I put my hands on her shoulders and looked her dead in the eyes. "Can you forget I ever said that? I honestly don't know that it's true. I have no clue what I'd do if that situation were to occur." The closer I got to Rebel, the more I doubted I'd allow Tara back in my life at all.

A slight smile curved her lips to one side. "Harman, I know you said you didn't love her, but I think you may have some feelings for her that you've hidden even from yourself. No one leaves an open door for someone they don't care about."

"Well, I guess I care about her." I could admit that. "I don't like seeing what she's doing to herself and our son. We went through a lot together; we raised a baby together. That's had its effects on us both."

"Ask yourself this," she said with a serious expression, "if you never saw her face again, would it matter to you?"

"Of course, it would matter to me." I didn't want my son to lose his mother. "I love Eli, that's why it would matter to me."

"Say what you want to, Harman." Rebel turned away to walk into the dressing room. "News of us *will* affect her—even if only in the same way you felt about her first boyfriend—and I don't want that to spoil their time together next weekend. So, for this week, keep it on the DL, will ya?"

I'd never contemplated what Tara would do or feel if I ever found anyone I was romantically interested in. If she did get jealous or upset, how would I feel about that?

Would it mean that Tara had managed to love me at some point in our marriage? And if so, would that mean we could have had the family I'd always wanted for our son?

And where would Rebel be in all that?

12

REBEL

STANDING in line at the movie theater the next afternoon, I had just as hard a time as Harman did at keeping my hands to myself. The man made my blood run hot.

Eli's excitement over the movie had us chuckling as we watched him throw up his hands. "And there's a huge warlock, and he's got special powers. More special than anyone else. Only he's blind." He looked up at his father with a serious expression. "Cause no one's perfect, not even a warlock!"

"Hey, Eli!" another little boy shouted. "Wow! I'm glad you came, too."

"Hey, Jason!" Eli looked at me. "It's my best friend, Rebel. 'Member I told ya about him?"

The kid ran up to Eli as his mother ambled along behind him. "Hi, I'm Jason's mother, Patricia." She held out her hand for me to shake. "And you must be the extraordinary veterinarian Eli's been talking about. It's a pleasure to finally meet you."

Harman nodded at her. "Has he been chewing your ear off, Patricia?"

"He has." She smiled at me. "Apparently, you're just about the best thing that's ever happened to the kid. I volunteer at the school, so I'm with them a lot. I've got the 'in' on what's happening with all the kids in Jason and Eli's class."

Eli tugged on his dad's pant leg. "Can I sit with Jason, Dad? Please."

Harman ran his hand through Eli's hair. "I'm sure his mother has her hands full with Jason. You sit with me, 'kay?"

"I'd actually love it if you'd let him sit with us," Patricia was quick to let him know. "That way those two can talk to each other about the movie, instead of Jason talking my ear off throughout the whole thing."

"Hey, can Eli spend the night?" Jason asked his mother.

I stood there, feeling a little on edge. If he got to spend the night at his friend's, then there wouldn't be anything stopping me and Harman from having our first night alone. And I knew exactly what that meant.

"If it's okay with his father," she said.

I looked at Harman with as much hope in my eyes as the two little boys. He caught my expression and smiled. "I think that'll be okay. I'll give the maid a call and have her drop off an overnight bag at your place." He looked at me. "They live two streets over."

"They do?" I looked at Jason. "Are you into animals as much as Eli is, Jason?"

"I like them. I have a cat. Not me, really. Mom has a cat." He looked up at his mom. "I'd like a dog."

"I bet you would," she said, then shrugged. "But I'm not into dogs. I'm a cat person."

"Well, Jason, if you'd ever like to come to my house after school, you can help Eli feed the animals I keep there." I looked at his mother. "You could drop him off, and I could take him home if that's okay with you."

"Sounds fantastic. An hour or so of alone time after school," she sighed. "Sounds kind of like heaven, I think."

Harman looked at me. "Well, since Eli's joining them for the movie, how about we take off and find something *we'd* like to do?"

That sounded an awful lot like he was asking me out in front of all of them. But I couldn't find it in me to actually care. "Sounds great."

Harman told Eli to behave and gave Patricia his thanks for looking after his son, and then the two of us took off. I felt a little giddy as we got into his car. He looked at me with the sexiest grin I'd ever seen. "Looks like our time has arrived."

My body tensed as goosebumps broke out over my skin. "Looks like it, doesn't it?"

"I think we should go out and eat a nice, expensive lunch," he suggested as he pulled out of the parking lot.

I looked at my sweater and jeans. "Um, I think I'll need to change for that."

"If I take you home first, we'll never get to eat." He took one hand off the steering wheel, running his fingers up my leg. "We'll grab a bite, then head home. I'm suddenly in a rush to get you there. I just had a new bedroom set delivered a few days ago. You don't have to worry about sleeping in the same bed she did."

I hadn't worried about that at all, actually—in fact, I hadn't even thought of it. And having sex in his house, a house that was full of his staff, didn't sound great. "While I'm glad you got yourself a new bedroom set, I think I'd feel more comfortable at my place."

"Done." He didn't bat an eye at that. "Whatever makes you feel comfortable, that's what I want, too." He looked over at me as he stopped at a light. "Instead of hauling ass to grab a bite and then rushing to your bedroom, how about a real date?"

More waiting?

"Harman, I'd love to go out with you." I needed to be honest with him. "But right now, my insides are quivering. My panties are getting wetter by the minute, and I don't think I've ever been this ready to have sex in my life."

"Fuck," I heard him whisper. He turned at the next light. "You've got food at your place. I'm right there with you, Rebel. We can figure out food later."

Glad to be on the same page, I said, "I can't think of anything I want to eat anyway. Well, besides you."

His eyes went wide as I leaned over to kiss his neck. He hit the gas just a little bit harder. "I think I'm going to really like dating you, Rebel."

"I think I'm going to like dating you, too." Moving my hand over his thigh, I rounded the corner to see how big the bulge in his pants was. I was not disappointed. "Oh, baby. I think something of this magnitude requires some special attention."

His lips quirked to one side. "This isn't anywhere near what I'd imagined. I saw us eating, maybe even going out dancing a little, and then going to my place. There'd be candles and soft music. I'd lay you on my bed, then undress you slowly."

"Sounds sweet." I moved my hand over his bulge. "I've got candles and soft music at my place. It's almost as good as what you wanted."

Pulling into my drive, he looked at me as he ran his hand over my cheek. "You, the bed, the candles, and the music were the best parts of that fantasy anyway. Now, come on. We've got a lot of firsts to get to."

My hand shook as I unlocked my door and I laughed nervously. "God, look what you're doing to me."

He put his hand over mine to steady it. "You think you're shaking now. Just wait."

We got the door open and barely made it over the threshold before he pushed me up against the wall—and our mouths finally met. My hands went to his hair, and his hands felt like they were everywhere, moving all over my body.

He picked me up, and I wrapped my legs around him as our mouths collided over and over in an explosion of passion. His swollen hardness moved against that most sensitive part of me, making me wetter and wetter with each grind.

Our movements completely in sync, our clothing left our bodies without either of us being aware of it. Suddenly we were naked, our bare skin rubbing together, our bodies falling to the floor with a need neither of us could deny any longer.

My eyes locked on his as he pushed my legs open then laid his body over mine. Nothing else existed around me but him—not the cold tile on my back, not the hard floor that dug into my shoulders—it was only me and Harman. The tip of his cock nudged at the precipice of my pulsing cunt, and I arched my body to get him where I needed him the most.

"Easy," he whispered hoarsely. "I want to look into your eyes when you feel me inside you for the first time."

I moved my hands up to hold either side of his face. "Let me look into yours, too, then. I didn't know there were men like you out there, Harman."

Slowly, he pushed into me. "I didn't know there were women out there like you either, Rebel. Gorgeous, brilliant, generous, sweet, and kind."

"Sexy?" I asked, never having felt sexier than I did at that moment.

He moved into me a little more, and I groaned at the way the heat spread through me. "Sexy as sin." He eased himself further into me, spreading me, making me burn with an intensity that would've hurt, had it been anything other than him who'd evoked it.

I moved my hands to his shoulders, digging my nails into his flesh. "God, stretching to fit you is going to make me come already." My body rocked with a mini climax.

Moving slowly, he reached down to where our bodies joined and spread the juices my body gave him. "Shit, Rebel! God, you're amazing." He moved faster, my body quaking harder around his cock with every thrust.

I'd had no idea it could be this good, and we'd just started. My mind shattered, I could barely breathe as he took me from one climax to another before he finally gave me that final thing I craved. His orgasm shook my entire body as he made the sexiest groan I'd ever heard, "Baby, fuck."

He collapsed on top of me, making me feel like I'd satisfied him so completely. It made me feel like a woman I'd never been before—a powerful, sexual woman, who'd brought her man to a place beyond words.

Panting, he rested his body on mine for a moment. Our hearts pounded against the other's as our sweat combined on our glistening bodies. His lips pressed against my neck as he moved off me. I held him for a second. "Don't go yet. I've never felt this before."

"You mean the connection?" He nodded as his lips moved up my neck. "Me neither. I never knew sex could be like this."

"Do you think it will always be like this?" I'd read somewhere that waiting to have sex could make it all the hotter when it finally happened, and I thought that would maybe explain the explosive connection we'd just had.

"I think I'd like to find out." He pulled his body off mine, and I immediately felt lost without him. But then he reached down, picked me up, and then headed down the hallway. "After a shower. Or maybe during the shower. And then after the shower, too. I have a feeling we won't be getting much sleep tonight."

Resting my head on his broad chest, I had the same feeling. "At some point, we'll have to get something to eat and drink." I lifted my head, then kissed him as he took me to the bathroom adjacent to my bedroom on the other side of the house.

Pulling my mouth off his, it suddenly occurred to me that he knew my home a bit more intimately than I'd realized. "Have you been sneaking around my house, Harman?"

"What?" He grinned sheepishly. "You mean, like checking out your bedroom while you made Eli and I some bowls of ice cream last week?"

"I see now." I kissed him again. "Your place is too big for me to snoop around. I would get lost for sure if I'd tried that."

"Most likely." He put me down, then leaned in to start the shower. "I had a purpose for my nosiness."

"And that was?" I ran my hand over his perfect ass as he leaned over.

"I wanted to see where you slept so I could picture you in your bed as I ravaged you in my sexual fantasies." He turned to pick me up again. "I couldn't have all of my fantasies taking place in my bedroom. That would be boring."

"And how many of these fantasies did you have?" I asked, feeling even sexier knowing that he'd had more than one about me.

"I've lost count." He pushed me up against the tiled wall, our bodies flush once more. "And to be honest, the real you is a much better lover than the fantasy you."

I'd never been called any sort of lover at all. To hear this man say something like that, and to see the lusty look in his eyes gave me a confidence I hadn't had before. "Well, I've got something that the real me has never done before. I've never wanted to before. But I want to with you, Harman."

"I'm sure I'll be into it," he said with a nod. "What is it?"

I chewed on my lip, suddenly feeling a little bit shy—despite the fact that I was pressed skin to skin with the man. "Well, I've never given a blow job. What better place than in this shower to learn? And who better to learn with?"

13

HARMAN

AFTER SPENDING JUST one night in Rebel's bed, I felt like I was walking around on air the rest of the weekend. Sunday, we spent the day together with Eli and went out for dinner before I took Rebel home. With Eli sitting in the car, I didn't even get a goodnight kiss. It left me feeling empty.

After putting my son to bed, I called Rebel, not having had enough of her despite spending the whole day with her. I knew not even one of our long phone conversations would be enough for me anymore. When I finally fell asleep, I dreamed about her all night long.

Waking on Monday morning feeling groggy, I made my rounds at the hospital as usual then went to get a large cup of coffee to help get me through the morning. Finding my associate, Doctor Jonas Kerr, sitting at a table alone in the cafeteria, I went to join him. "How's the morning treating you, Jonas?"

"I've got a board meeting this afternoon, and I'm not looking forward to it." He ran his hand down the extra-large coffee on the table in front of him. "Hence the need for all this coffee."

"Sure glad I haven't been asked to be on the board." I took a seat.

"I've got my hands full as it is, what with my son." I thought about Rebel. "And now a girlfriend, too."

He looked at me with a grin. "So, you've finally moved on from the ex, huh?"

"I wasn't staying away from other women because I was hung up on her." Tara had never been the reason for my lack of a love life. I took a sip of the hot coffee. "This woman just slipped under my skin somehow when I wasn't even looking. She's actually perfect for me—and my son."

Jonas's expression shifted to one of concern. "You mean you've already introduced her to your kid?"

"No. He was the one who introduced her to me." I thought back to that very first day when I saw Rebel walk out of her house. "She pretty much grabbed onto my heart and held it from the first time we met. She's our new neighbor. My son went to introduce himself to her —which was not like him at all—and they hit it off from the get-go."

"She's *your* neighbor?" he asked. "So, she's got tons of money, too?"

"No." I thought about the little car she drove and how surprised she'd be if I bought her something new and insanely expensive. "She's still struggling to pay off her student loans, actually. She's a vet. The lady next door sold off her carriage house for a really low price. That's how she's living in my neighborhood."

"How's the ex taking the news?" He picked up his coffee, taking a long drink.

"She's not entirely aware of our budding relationship. And neither is my son." Something told me Eli wouldn't mind at all.

"Maybe you two should wait a while—make sure things are going to work out—before you go telling either of them," he advised.

He had no idea how much time we'd spent together with Eli though. "If we don't let my son know soon, I think our actions will tell him before our words can. We're having a hard time keeping our hands off each other at this point."

"New love," he said then sighed. "Man, it's been a while since I've experienced that."

I'd known the man for a couple of years, and as far as I knew, he'd never had anyone permanent in his life. "Being the general surgeon around here must take up most of your time. Maybe you should use your position on the board to get more help around this place. Our staff could use a boost, don't you think?"

"I do." He shoved his hand through his dark hair. "One of the items on the agenda is about another neurosurgeon. He's been out of practice for about a year, and he's petitioned the board, asking to work here at Saint Christopher's. But he's got a few issues that have some of the board members concerned."

"Like?" I asked.

"Like, he's had a rough couple of years in his personal life. He lost his wife to cancer a little over a year ago." He looked grim, taking a big drink of coffee after a pause. "And he's got a three-year-old, too. I'm one of the skeptics. I'm not sure he's ready for all this."

My heart went out to the poor kid. Losing a mother must be horrible for a child. Eli was affected by his mother's absence, and she wasn't even dead. What would it be like to know—without a doubt— that you'd never see your mother again?

"I can't imagine how the man is dealing with that." And I was glad I didn't have to deal with that myself. "It feels hard enough just dealing with an ex who doesn't seem to remember her son's existence."

"Kids need their mothers." He looked at his nearly empty cup. "I think that's what has me on the fence with this guy. His kid needs him around. If he's working here, he'll be away from home more than he's at home. You know how that goes, Harman."

I did know, but I also knew that a good parent could put what matters the most first when they had to. "If I were you, I'd talk to the guy and figure out what his plans are. See if he plans on hiring someone to care for his child, or if he's got other family to look after the boy. At least then, the kid has a stable home life. That's important. I can always help the guy adjust to life as a hard-working, single father. Plus we've got another neurosurgeon on board here already.

This place doesn't have to consume his entire life the way it does yours, Jonas."

"Maybe I should keep on the lookout for another general surgeon, huh?" he said with a chuckle.

"I have the feeling if you ever met someone special yourself, then you'd figure out pretty quickly how to juggle this job and a personal life." I felt my pocket vibrating and got up to answer the call. "I'll talk to you later, Jonas. Take it easy."

I felt a smile curve my lips as I looked down and saw Rebel's name. I couldn't ever recall a time that a call from Tara made my heart skip a beat.

I answered the call and before I could even get out a greeting, Rebel asked, "Do you miss me yet?"

"Damn straight." Just hearing her voice made my cock stir. "I can't wait to get my hands on you again, Doctor Saxe."

"I can't wait for that either." She sighed with what I hoped were great memories of our one night together. "I'm still sore from our last session. I think I need a little more practice to become accustomed to all this activity. So, when do you think that'll happen?"

"If Tara takes Eli, then this coming weekend you'll get a full two nights and three days of my attention." I crossed my fingers that Tara would come through this time.

"I've been thinking, and I wanted to talk to you about this," she said. "I know I've been the one saying not to tell Eli about us, but I'm starting to feel kind of like we're hiding something. And I don't want Eli to think either of us wants to hide stuff from him. So, what do you say to telling him about us?"

"It would certainly help things when we're all together, wouldn't it?" I hated how I couldn't even hold her hand when Eli was around. "I could stop by on my way home. He'll probably still be at your place anyway. We could tell him together this evening if you want to."

"I do." She made a little moaning sound that sent a chill through me. "It's not fair to hide things from your son just because I'm afraid of how his mother will react. She's the one who left. She had to know that one day you'd find someone."

"I agree." I knew it would take time for everyone to adjust. Might as well start doing it. "Tara might be a little surprised, but I doubt she'll be that taken aback. She has heard Eli's daily reports of his days, and you and I are a big part of that."

"Yeah, I think it's best to be honest," she said. "And I'd like to be able to kiss your cheek and have you wrap your arm around my shoulders in front of people without it being a big deal."

"That sounds good to me, too." It sounded better than good, but I didn't want to go overboard. "So, I'll be over later, and we'll let him know. Anyway, how's work going today?"

"A Rottweiler came in after being hit by a car, so that was horrific for a while. But I managed to get him stitched up, and he's resting comfortably." She laughed a little. "One of the vet techs took a pretty good bite to his arm. He cried like a girl. Then I found out it was his first dog bite, and I stopped laughing at him and bandaged him up good. I don't think he was ready for that to happen."

"That sounds more like the Rebel I know." There was so much to admire about the woman—she was so caring and empathetic. "So, how about I bring home Chinese tonight? We can eat dinner together at your place."

"Sounds good to me. No cooking, no cleaning, just eating and hanging with my boys—sounds like heaven to me." I heard someone call her name in the background and knew our talk had come to an end. "Gotta go, babe. They just brought in another dog that's been hit by a car. That's the third one. I don't know what's going on today, but I sure hope it stops now."

"Good luck, baby. See you around six. I'll miss you until then," I let her know.

"Same here. Bye, Harman."

Now we just have to tell Eli about us. Why does that scare me a little?

14

REBEL

As soon as I walked in my front door, I heard a knock on the back one. "Rebel, it's Eli! I'm here."

Unlocking the door, I saw Eli with his friend Jason, both of them standing there with smiles on their faces. Moppy strolled around the backyard, saying hi in his own way to the other animals in cages. "This was our last day of school," Eli told me. "Now we don't go back until a week from today."

"Yeah, next Monday we gotta go back," Jason said as he hopped up and down. "So, we can help you every day, even in the mornings if you want."

"You guys might have vacation, but I still have to go to work. I've only got Thursday—Thanksgiving Day—off." It would be fantastic if I didn't have to worry about feeding the animals in the mornings for a week, though. "There's another twenty for each of you for feeding and watering these guys every morning this week. That would be a great relief for me, so thank you for suggesting it."

Stepping out the back door, I saw the kids had already taken care of watering all the animals. "We just need you to put the food out here, so we can get to it," Eli told me. "I think if you put it into a big garbage can with a lid on it, nothing will be able to get into it, and we can leave it out."

"Great idea." I walked around the side of the house to the garage. "I've got one in the garage I haven't even used. It would be perfect."

Rolling the large door up, I watched the boys as their eyes went wide. "All this space," Jason said, then looked at me. "There's nowhere in our whole place that has this much empty space."

"Well, I haven't accumulated much since moving in." I tapped my chin as I looked at just how bare the garage was. "I suppose it'll start getting filled up once I buy Christmas decorations. After the new year, I'll stack those things up in here to store them." I pointed at the empty black garbage container. "Eli, will you grab that? It's got wheels, so you can just pull it outside."

Eli did as I asked, and I closed the door back up. Jason seemed just as happy as Eli with his new job. "I've never had a job before. It's pretty cool." Shoving his hands in his pockets, he shivered as a cool breeze swept through the backyard. "It's getting chilly again."

"It's going to be a cold Thanksgiving this year, from what I've seen on the weather channel." I opened the back door. "I'll grab the bags of food, and you guys can put them into the container after you feed everyone out here. I'm going to turn on the warming lamps for them. I'll cover some of them up with blankets later on."

As we tended the animals, I found my heart racing as I thought about Eli's reaction later to our news. I couldn't wait to tell him; I thought he'd likely be thrilled that I'd be even more a part of his life than I'd already been these last few weeks.

After we finished, we all loaded up in my car—even Eli's new dog —so I could take Jason home. "Two streets over, right?"

Eli pointed the way as the two of them sat in the back seat. "Take a right."

I turned and went two streets down, stopping in front of another magnificent mansion. "Jason, I hope you know the code to the gate."

"It's my birthday," he said, then nothing else.

I sat there with the window rolled down, my finger hovering over the keypad. "And that is?"

The boys cracked up, then Jason said, "Oh, yeah, you don't know when my birthday is. September sixth, two-thousand, ten."

Punching that in using only numbers, I got the gates to open. Driving up the curvy drive, I couldn't help but marvel at the entire property. "What a beautiful place, Jason. It must be great growing up here."

"I guess." He looked out the window. "I just wish Mom and Dad had had me when they had my brother and sisters. They waited fifteen years after the triplets before having me. All of them have moved away, so I'm all alone here."

Eli shrugged. "At least you got a brother and some sisters. I ain't got nothin' at all."

At eight years old, I knew even if either of his parents ever had more kids, Eli would probably never be as close to them as he would've been had he had a brother or sister when he was younger. It made me feel a little bad for the boy. I had no idea how lonely it would've been, growing up without a sibling.

"See you tomorrow, Jason." I stopped at the ornate front entrance. "Tell your mom hi for me."

"Okay, I will." Jason hopped out of the car, waving goodbye to us.

We waved back as I drove away. "Your dad's going to bring Chinese food for us for dinner tonight. So, I'm taking you back to my place, Eli."

"Cool." He smiled as he looked out the window. "Are you going to spend Thanksgiving with us, Rebel?"

"I might spend some of it with you guys." I had plans to go to my family's and wondered if I should invite Eli and Harman to come with me.

"We always have our Thanksgiving meal at lunchtime," he said. "When do you guys have it?"

"Usually around then." I frowned a little. "And your grandparents are going to be at your place." I'd just remembered them saying that. "I guess I won't see you until I get back around dinner time."

We pulled to a stop in my driveway and got out of the car. "It would be nice if your family could come to our house, too."

I ran my hand through his hair, which had already gotten a bit shaggy. "Who knows? Maybe someday." Maybe someday Harman and I would be even more to each other. One day, he and I might even be living in that big house together. But that wasn't going to be happening anytime soon.

Just as we got inside the house, my cell rang. When I pulled it out of the pocket of my scrubs, Eli saw Harman's name on the screen. "There's Dad. Can you remind him about the eggrolls, please? I like those the best, and sometimes he forgets them."

"Will do," I answered the call. "Hello there, Doctor Hunter."

"Hey, I wanted to call before I picked up the food. What's your favorite Chinese dish?" he asked.

"All of them." I winked at Eli as he watched me. "Especially eggrolls, so get plenty of those please."

"Hmm," he hummed. "You wouldn't be putting in an extra order of egg rolls for Eli, now would you?"

"Who, me?" I said with a high voice. "Not me."

Eli whispered, "And don't forget the fortune cookies."

"Oh, yeah," I added, "and please don't forget the fortune cookies."

"Okay," I could hear the smile in his voice. "You don't want anything special? You're going to leave this up to me?"

"It's all up to you, babe." I put my hand over my mouth, catching my slip-up when I saw Eli's furrowed brow.

"Oh, shit," Harman hissed. "Bye."

He hung up, leaving me standing there with no idea what to tell Eli. Thankfully, I didn't have to say anything as Eli just went to sit on the sofa and picked up the remote. "Can I find a movie for us all to watch, Rebel?"

"Great idea." I went to the kitchen to get out plates and make us something to drink. And mostly to keep some distance between us until his father got there. I didn't want to tell Eli about us on my own.

After busying myself for a half hour, Harman finally came through the front door. "Dinner is served."

Eli jumped up off the sofa. "Good, I'm starving to death."

I met them at the dining room table. "Hi, there. Smells awesome."

Harman pulled the containers out as he looked at me with a curious expression. "So, what've you two been doing?"

"I picked out a movie for us all to watch after dinner," Eli said. "Are we gonna hang out for a while, Dad?"

"Well, since you don't have school tomorrow, I thought we might hang out," Harman said.

I spooned the contents of the containers onto three plates then passed them out. "Sounds good to me, guys. I'd love the company."

Eli picked up an eggroll, taking a big bite out of it. "Yummy!"

Harman and I took our seats, and we all ate without saying much. We made small talk, mostly about what Eli would be doing over the holiday.

"Hey, do you want to come to work with me one day, Eli?" I asked, thinking he'd love that.

His jaw dropped. "Could I?"

"If it's okay with your dad." I looked at Harman for his answer.

Nodding, he said, "I guess it would be fine, seeing as you're my girlfriend now."

Eli smiled. "I knew it!" He laughed as he pointed at us. "Dad and Rebel, sitting in a tree."

Harman leaned over and pressed his lips against my cheek. "Well, I'm glad that cat's out of the bag now."

"Yuck!" Eli squealed. "Girls have cooties, Dad."

I tossed a fortune cookie at the kid. "We do not!"

Harman sat back against his chair. "Well, I'll take them if she's got them."

Eli looked back and forth at his father and me. "I'm glad. I like it when we're all together. It's better."

Harman agreed, "I think so, too." His eyes went to mine. "Rebel, you make things better. I hope you know that."

"You guys make my life better, too." I thought about how boring my life had been before I met them. "I thought my life was fine, but then I realized how dull it had really been after I met you two."

Eli looked at me with knowing eyes. "It's kind of like we were all meant to be together."

"Profound for such a young boy," Harman mused as he ran his hand over his son's head.

"Time for another trim before we watch the movie, I think," I said as I watched them.

"I think I need one, too," Harman said, then looked at me. "I want to look sharp for the holiday. And I'd love it if you'd join us."

"I can't." It didn't make me happy to have to decline. "I've got to go see my family. We do the meal at lunchtime, and Eli's told me you guys do it then, too. And your parents will be coming for that."

"We'll do ours in the evening, then, if it means you can be there." Harman reached across the table to take my hand. "I want you to be there. I'll change the time if that's what it takes to make that happen. It's no big deal, you know."

Although I didn't think he needed to do that, I loved that he would. "I almost want to tell you not to, but the truth is, that makes me extremely happy that you would do that to make sure I'm included in the holiday with you guys."

"So you're saying yes," he didn't ask, just stated. "Because I know I want to spend that time with you and Eli and my parents. It won't be the same without you."

Eli's eyes glistened as he looked at his father. "Just like a real family, right, Dad?"

Harman's thumb moved across my knuckles, and my insides melted at the look he gave me. "Yeah, Little Buddy. It'll feel like a real Thanksgiving this year. Waiting a few hours for Rebel won't hurt us a bit, will it?"

"Nope," Eli agreed.

I'd never had anyone look at me the way those two did. It stirred something deep inside of me—something that had laid undisturbed until that moment.

The next evening we had the HOA meeting, and I was a bundle of nerves.

I stepped into the garage—a ten-car garage, milling with catering staff—with Harman at my side. Patricia waved at us. "Come over here and sit with us."

Harman took my hand in his, making sure everyone knew we were together. "Hey, Patricia. Thanks for the invite."

He pulled my chair out, and I sat down as I felt all eyes turn to me. "I've dreaded this," I admitted in a whisper.

She pushed a plate full of food toward us. "No reason to dread this. It's more of a get together than a meeting. So, are you two finally official, or what?"

I looked at Harman as he quickly said, "Yes, we are." His eyes cut to two men who looked our way. "Make sure Jack and Bill know that, too."

When I looked at the men he'd spoken about, they both waved at me. And I laughed as Harman took our clasped hands to wave back at them. "Harman!"

"What? They need to know." He kissed my hand in front of everyone and just like that, our relationship was out there for our neighbors to see. No more hiding from anyone.

But there was still that one person who didn't know yet. And I still felt worried about how she'd take the news.

15

HARMAN

THE THANKSGIVING HOLIDAY passed in a happy blur, and both Eli and I had a better time than either of us could remember. My parents had pulled me to the side to let me know they adored Rebel and were happy about our budding relationship.

Things couldn't have been better. And when Friday came, Eli got a call from his mother telling him she'd be there to pick him up at four that afternoon. She also wanted to know if Eli would take her to meet Rebel, the other woman in his life.

I'd planned on being there for that meeting. I didn't think Rebel should have to do that on her own. But an emergency surgery had me running late, and I found I couldn't make it after all.

At the tail end of the surgery, I was supervising an intern as she stitched up our patient and looked at the clock on the wall. *Four o'clock exactly.*

I wondered if Tara was at my home already and on time to pick up our son. Or had she flaked again?

The minutes went by slowly, and I kept looking back and forth from the patient to the clock. When four-thirty came around, I felt a twist in my gut, as if my body was sensing that Rebel and Tara were meeting at that very moment.

Would they be cordial to one another in front of Eli? Or would one of them feel threatened and lash out at the other? Not over me, but over Eli. That boy thought Rebel hung the moon and that showed in his eyes. And Eli had been terribly disappointed by his mother, and that showed in his eyes, too. I also knew how protective Rebel felt about Eli.

"He's good to go, Doctor Hunter," the intern informed me.

"Okay, take him to recovery, and I'll have Doctor Kerr check on him when he comes out of anesthesia. I've got to get going." I left the OR, hoping I could make it back before the actual meeting took place.

After changing into jeans and a sweater, I headed for my car, pulling my cell out of the pocket of my jeans. I dialed Rebel, wanting to find out what I'd missed.

"Hey, babe," she answered.

"Hey." I clicked the fob to unlock my car as a gust of wind whipped by me. "Is she there?"

"Not anymore. They just left," she let me know.

"And how'd it go?" I got into the driver's seat, turned the car ignition, then cranked up the heater. "Damn, it's cold today."

"I know. I've got a fire going in the fireplace. It's nice and toasty in here." She took a deep breath. "And it went okay. She was nice. And she even told me she appreciated my advice and the time I spent with her son."

"That was nice of her." Relief washed over me. "So, it went well. And Eli was happy?"

"Beyond happy," she sounded happy about that, too. "He was so excited to introduce us to each other. I couldn't stop smiling at how excited he was."

"Good. I'm glad it's all working out." I had one more thing I wanted to know. "Did you or Eli tell her about us?"

"No," came her quick answer. "It didn't feel like the right time for that, and I suppose Eli felt the same way. Neither of us said one word about you."

"Well, I guess that's okay. It's not exactly her business anyway." I turned to get on the highway. "Mom and Dad left this morning, and I gave the staff a three-day weekend, starting today. My place will be empty. What do you say to staying the weekend with me?"

"Hell yeah!" I heard her moving around. "I'll get packed, and you can pick me up on your way by."

"Sounds great. See you in fifteen minutes." It felt good to have someone to spend time with while Eli was away. During the past couple of years, it had always been lonely whenever Tara took him. But now I had Rebel to keep me company.

Things were looking up for Eli and me. Maybe Tara would even step up, now that she had a little competition for her son's affection.

I suppose a little competition is healthy.

Rebel came out of her house as soon as I pulled into her driveway, as if she'd been waiting and watching for me. Hurrying to the car, she got in and tossed her bag into the back seat. "Man, it's cold. If it's this cold now, what will Christmas be like?"

"We may get a snowy Christmas this year, I'm thinking. We're only ten degrees above freezing now." I took off, wanting to get her home and out of her clothes as quickly as possible.

She eyed me with a sexy smile on her lips. "Cuddling up with you while the snow falls outside sounds like heaven to me."

"Me, too." I pulled up inside the garage, then pushed the button to close it behind me. "At least we don't have to get out in the cold to get inside the house."

The place was always so eerily quiet when no one was home, and Rebel noticed it right away. "It feels almost empty. Where's Moppy?"

"The chef took him home for the weekend since Eli wasn't going to be here. She's fallen in love with the big old guy." Walking into the kitchen, I went to the fridge to grab the tray of meats, fruits, and cheeses the chef had made up for us to snack on. "It's been a while since no one's been home." I placed the tray on the bar then turned to gather my girl in my arms.

Our eyes met, then our lips did the same, and suddenly those snacks meant nothing to me. Lifting Rebel up, I put her on the bar, moving between her legs. Her arms moved around my neck as we got lost in one another.

Pulling up her shirt, I put my hands on her skin, loving the creamy smoothness of it. I pushed her bra up next, playing with her big tits until her nipples were hard as rocks. When that wasn't enough, I forced her to lie back on the granite top so I could taste her.

Her eyes soft and glazed, she watched me lean over to take a nipple in my mouth as I played with the other. Her moan moved me in ways nothing ever had.

As I sucked, licked, and nibbled her tasty tit, I thought about the fact that I hadn't even offered her a bite to eat before feasting on her myself. Pulling my mouth off her, I asked, "You hungry?" Then I realized that sounded a little bad-mannered. "Not for me. For food." I shoved my hand through my hair. "Ugh! You get me so—"

"So out of sorts?" she asked with a grin. "And no, I'm not hungry. Thanks for asking. Now come back here and get back to what you were doing. That was blowing my mind."

All I could do was look down at her. For nearly nine years, I'd been with only one woman. A woman I felt no real connection to in all that time. Tara had never told me that anything I did blew her mind. "Yesterday, when we were saying what we're thankful for, I wanted to say how thankful I am for you, Rebel."

Reaching up, she grabbed me by my shirt, pulling it off me. "And I am thankful for you, Doctor Hunter." Her hands moved over my six-pack then up to my pecs and finally settled on my biceps. "And for more than just this outstanding body you've built."

Running my hand through her silky hair, I whispered, "You're growing on me. Like a seed that blew in on a spring breeze, you're growing on me."

"I like that." Her fingers trailed down my arm to take my hand. She pulled it up, sucking on my index finger.

She'd practiced a new skill on me the last time we'd been together. And it looked as if she'd like to practice that new skill a bit more. I unzipped my jeans as I tossed my sneakers off, letting my pants drop to the floor seconds later. Rebel's eyes sparkled as she climbed off the bar to get on her knees in front of me.

Looking up at me, she slowly pulled down my black boxer briefs, releasing my long, hard cock. "So, you did like what I did last time? I was worried you were just saying that, so you didn't hurt my feelings."

"I'm not prone to giving false praise, baby." I put my hands on her shoulders as I leaned back against the bar. "This time, I'll stop you before I blow." I looked at the hardwood floor. "Do you think you'll have a problem staying on your knees for me?"

She shook her head. "Not a bit." Licking her lips, she wrapped her hands around my cock then kissed the tip gently before licking it like a lollipop.

When she took the whole thing into her hot mouth, I growled with satisfaction. "Yes, baby. Take it all in."

Moving slowly, she bobbed back and forth, sucking lightly as she did so. The woman turned me inside out. Looking down at her, watching her suck me off, I couldn't recall ever seeing anything so beautiful in my life.

Tangling my hands in her hair, I tilted her head slightly so she would look me in the eye. "Rebel, you're the most gorgeous woman I've ever laid eyes on. What you do to me feels unreal at times."

Rebel's mouth quivered as she moaned and closed her eyes in pleasure, and I nearly lost it then. Panting, I pulled her back, letting her know she'd taken me to the edge and had to stop.

Smiling up at me, she moved back a bit while still on her knees before getting up and pulling off her shirt and bra as I watched. Then she shimmied out of her jeans after kicking off her flats. Naked now, she got back to the floor on her hands and knees.

My body shook with desire as I moved to get behind her. Her firm ass high in the air, she wiggled it at me. "I'm ready for you, Doctor," she purred.

"You're such a bad girl." I smacked her ass. "Making your doctor fuck you raw—you shouldn't be doing this to me."

"But it's the only medicine that makes me better." Rebel looked at me over her shoulder, a pout on her swollen lips. "Give it to me good,

Doc. I'm sick with the need to feel your cock buried deep inside of my aching pussy."

"You been watching porn, baby?" I smiled at her, breaking character as I thrust into her.

She gasped at the force of my penetration. "No, reading naughty books at work." I smacked her ass again as I rammed into her hard. "Damn, why does that feel so good?" she moaned.

Since it felt good, I did it again and again until her hot cunt dripped all around my cock, squeezing me until I blew into her. Our harsh breathing reverberated off the kitchen walls as we tried to catch our breaths.

Lifting her to her feet, I picked her up bridal style then carried her up to my bedroom. "It looks like it's going to be another one of those nights, Rebel. I can't get enough of you."

Hanging onto my neck, she laid her head on my chest. "I've needed another one of those kinds of nights." She kissed my cheek as my foot hit the first stair. "And we can turn this night into two!"

If this weekend doesn't kill us, it'll only make us stronger!

16

REBEL

Waking up in Harman's bed was heavenly. The huge bed felt even bigger as we cuddled in the middle of it. Sunlight came streaming in through the curtains as it took over the morning sky.

When I moved out of Harman's arms to get up to use the bathroom, he growled a little and pulled me tighter—as if he didn't want to let me go at all. "I've gotta pee, babe."

He let me go reluctantly, then turned over to his other side, falling back to sleep right away. We'd made love until late in the night. I had my doubts that we'd have the energy to do much that day. I envisioned staying in bed most of the day, trying to recover—and then doing it all over again.

I limped to the bathroom, never feeling so sore in my life. I tried not to groan at the stiffness, but a small noise came out of me as I made my way to the adjacent bathroom.

Once inside, I closed the door and let out a louder moan. "Aw, man."

If I wanted to be able to walk properly again, I had to get into a hot tub of water. I started a bath before using the bathroom, then brushing my teeth. Thankful for taking the five minutes it took to put my bag in the bathroom the night before, I grabbed my shampoo and conditioner, so I could wash my hair.

As I soaked in the tub, I thought I might go downstairs after getting dressed and make us some breakfast. I hoped to impress Harman by showing off my culinary skills, my breakfast dishes being my best.

After getting ready, I peeked out the bathroom door to find Harman still fast asleep. Tiptoeing out of the room, I went downstairs to see what I could make.

Of course, the kitchen pantry had everything one could imagine. So I decided on a ham and cheese quiche. I threw together some hash browns on the side and grabbed a few biscuits that his chef had left in the fridge.

The coffee had just finished brewing, and I'd poured two glasses of juice when Harman walked into the kitchen, wearing only a robe. He looked so cute with his hair a mess. "You left me."

Holding my arms open, I gestured to the breakfast. "I wanted to make us breakfast."

"Look at my little Holly Homemaker." Closing in on me with a grin, he added. "I've brushed my teeth. How about a morning kiss?"

"I think I can handle that." His arms closed around me, enveloping me in his warm strength. "I liked waking up in your massive bed with you."

"I liked holding you all night." He kissed me softly, then pressed his forehead to mine. "I think it's going to be hard to go back to not doing that."

I didn't know what to say to that. When Eli came back home, it wouldn't be right for me to be stay over at night. But I kept that to myself. "We've got tonight, too. Unless you're giving me the boot."

"Never." He kissed me again.

My heart sped up as our kiss grew deeper. I had to end it before we took it too far, pulling my mouth away from his. "We've got to eat. We didn't eat a thing yesterday after lunch."

"You're right, Doctor Saxe." He let me go. "Let's get our grub on."

Plating up the food, I placed them on the table as Harman made us cups of coffee. "A splash of creamer in mine, please."

We sat down at the same time, and I loved the hungry expression he wore as he looked at his plate. "Yum, baby."

"Thank you." It thrilled me to no end that he liked the food I'd made. "You've got absolutely every ingredient anyone could ever need in here. It was pretty easy to come up with something."

Taking a bite of the quiche, he smiled. "So good."

I took a bite of mine then nodded. "Yes, it is."

"We should take my truck to get a Christmas tree today. That way we can put it up today and decorate it." He paused to take a sip of his coffee. "I've got loads of decorations my mother has picked out over the last couple of years. I keep it all in one of the downstairs empty bedrooms—Eli and I call it the Christmas room. You can go explore and see what we have to work with while I get myself cleaned up. We drop the tree off here, and I'll give my lawn guy a call to come set it up for us while we're out. Then we can shop for more decorations and a few presents. That way Eli will have a big surprise when he gets home tomorrow."

"And here I thought you and I would stay in bed all day today." I smiled at him over the rim of my coffee cup.

"Well, we can do that if you'd rather." He pulled one half of his robe away, so I could see him flex his pec. "You need a little more of this, baby?"

Laughing at him, I said, "I could use another dose. But to be honest, I really love your first idea. There's always tonight for more of...that," I said as my gaze roamed over the bit of flesh he'd bared.

After breakfast, I went to check out the Christmas room and found so many things that it made it hard to pick out what to use. All I knew for sure was that he didn't need to buy any more decorations.

I put the things I thought would look good in the front of the large room, which was meant to be someone's bedroom. With my cell in hand, I decided to venture around the place to become more familiar with it. I had my phone with me in case I got lost.

On the lower level, I counted four bedrooms and six baths, along with a bunch of other living spaces. And I knew there were even more rooms upstairs. I wondered how Harman and Eli could feel at home in the enormous place. They hadn't always lived this way, after all. It had to have taken some getting used to.

When Harman called me on my cell, I answered it right away. "Hi, I'm lost in your mansion."

"Take the first right. All rights lead back to the living room." He laughed. "Just kidding. Tell me where you are, and I'll come find you."

"There's a giant television," and I did mean *giant*. "And some theater seats, too." I looked around and saw a popcorn machine and a small bar. "How come we didn't just watch that movie Eli wanted to see in this place?"

"Because he likes to watch movies with other people." The door opened, and he stepped inside. "But you and I could catch a few flicks in here if you'd like."

I went to the bar and found it stocked. "How many stocked bars do you have in this place, Harman?"

Shaking his head, I knew he probably didn't have any clue. "I don't take care of all that, my housekeeper does. Well, she's more like a home manager than a housekeeper."

"This place is more for entertainment than living." I wanted to see more, to find a place that felt more like home. "Take me on a tour, Harman."

Looping his arm through mine, he led me away. "Eli and I typically use the small dining area just outside the kitchen. We watch television in the media room near the swimming pool room, which is the other room we use a lot. And then there are our bedrooms. His is across the hall from mine. Other than that, most of these rooms go unused."

I didn't say it, but I thought the extravagance of the place seemed a bit on the wasteful side. "Maybe we can find a place in here that feels more like home."

"There's this one place that I think is supposed to be servant's quarters." He opened a door, and it looked like an apartment inside.

The suite had one large room in front, and then a hallway behind it that led to a small kitchen with a bathroom on the other side. And two small bedrooms, too.

We looked at each other, both shaking our heads as I said, "Nah, too much like my old apartment."

"Yeah, that's what I think, too," he agreed. "Too small, and too much like our old place."

As we wandered around, he took me into a round room. "This is where I've had the Christmas tree set up the last two years."

"And what's behind those doors?" There were three in total.

"Come on—I'll show you." He led me to the first door and I found a library on the other side. It was packed with books of all kinds. Another door led to another large round room, but this one had an enormous skylight that lit up the space. I knew it would be remarkable at night, when the stars came out.

"Harman, why not make this the main living area? Looking up at the night sky would be insane." I pointed to the wall. "The curvature of the wall would be great for one of those televisions that curve, too. But this white furniture should be switched out with something else. Maybe something leather. You've got loads of furnishings here."

"I like the leather set in that room with all the windows that faces the back of the property." Harman looked around the room. "I've never considered this room as a living area. You're right, though, it would be an exceptional place to spend time."

Putting his arm around me, he gave me a squeeze. "If you want to put your touch on this place, it's welcomed, baby. Needed, even. It feels like living in a museum sometimes, having all these spaces that feel off limits."

"It's all yours, though." But I knew what he was talking about. The place didn't feel lived in. And he and Eli had been there for years already. "I'll help you break it in."

Arching one eyebrow, he smiled. "Great idea. We can break in each room one at a time."

Laughing, I took his hand. "Let's go find the perfect Christmas tree first. I can't wait to see Eli's face tomorrow when he sees what we've done."

Harman didn't move when I tugged him. Instead, he pulled me back, wrapping his arms around me. "I wonder why I've never met anyone like you before, Rebel Saxe. You wear your heart on your sleeve—a heart that's bigger than I can imagine. You adore my son."

"I do." I couldn't hide that.

"You treat him almost like he's your own child." He shook his head as if he couldn't understand that. "You don't *have* to do anything for him, yet you do all sorts of things. And you do it because you want to, not because you have to. Not because I ask you to."

"He's a great kid." I'd never known such a good kid.

"It's not a word I've said much in my life," he whispered as if it was a big secret, "the word *love*. Other than Eli, I've never said it to anyone. *No one*, Rebel."

"Are you trying to tell me that you love me, Harman?" My heart swelled.

"When I say it, I want you to know I really mean it. But it's getting more and more obvious that there's something building between us that feels a hell of a lot like that word."

I smiled, knowing exactly what he meant—because I felt it, too.

17

HARMAN

Sunday evening came, and I hated to see the weekend coming to an end. But everything had to end eventually. Rebel and I were in the kitchen cooking chili together when Eli called. "Hey, Little Buddy."

Rebel pulled out a knife, then set to work cutting up an onion. "Tell him to ask his mother if she'd like to join us for dinner when she drops him off," she whispered.

"Um." I didn't know if that was a good idea. "When are you going to be home?" I asked my son.

"Soon," Eli said. "And tell Rebel that's okay. We're on our way now."

"Okay, see you soon then." I swiped to end the call then put the phone down on the countertop. "He sounds a little sad or upset."

Rebel wiped tears out of her eyes as she sniffled. "That's not good. I wonder what happened."

Pulling her into my arms, I used a dish towel to wipe her eyes. "Let me finish cutting that up."

"Why?" she asked. "I'm already crying. Why should you get all teary over this onion, too?"

I didn't bother explaining, just took the knife away from her and moved her to the sink before turning on the cold water. "Stand here until the stinging goes away."

"Doctor's orders?" she asked with a laugh.

"Yes." I went to chop up the rest of the onion, doing it so quickly that the fumes couldn't bother me. Tossing the chopped onions into the chili simmering on the stove, I went to wash the knife and cutting board, Eli still heavy on my mind. "I wonder what happened."

It took another fifteen minutes before Eli came home. He came in the side door with his head low, looking tired and sad. "Hey, guys."

Rebel looked at him, and then watched me as I walked over to my son. Putting my arm around his shoulders, I asked, "Wanna tell me what happened?"

He looked up at me, then over at Rebel. "I don't want to hurt her feelings, Dad."

Rebel took the cue. "I've gotta go to the little girl's room." Exiting quickly, she left us alone.

"How about now, Eli? Wanna talk to me?" I asked.

He went to sit at the kitchen bar, then finally said, "I told Mom about you and Rebel. I thought she'd be happy. She said she liked Rebel after we left her house."

"When did you tell your mom about this?" I asked. I'd talked to him on Saturday, and he hadn't been upset.

"A little while ago." He sniffed the air. "Is that chili?"

"Yeah," I told him, moving back to the stove to give it a stir.

"I like chili. Is there cornbread, too?" he asked, looking a little happier, which made me feel better.

Maybe it's not as bad as he thinks.

I opened the oven to show him the pan of cornbread cooking inside. "There sure is."

"Good." He smiled. "That makes me feel a little better, Dad. Anyway, I told Mom about you and Rebel because I was pretty sure Rebel would be here when Mom brought me home. 'Cause I know you like spending time with her. And I didn't want Mom to be surprised."

"Sounds awfully mature of you, son." I was continually surprised at the thoughtful boy my son was turning out to be.

"Yeah, well, it didn't do what I thought it would." Then the sadness came over him again. "Mom cried. She ran out of the room and didn't come back for a long time. And when she did, she told me she was sad because she thought one day we'd be a family again."

"She shouldn't have done that." I felt fury building inside of me, but I tried to keep a calm face for Eli. "I'm sorry she did that to you. I'll talk to her about it."

"Please don't say anything else to make her cry, Dad. It broke my heart." He got up and went to the fridge to get a bottle of water.

I sat down, feeling like I might fall down. Hearing him say that seeing his mother cry had broken his heart, well... That nearly broke mine. "Okay, I won't then, Eli."

He took a long drink of the water bottle. "It's good to have some water finally. Mom has these new rules. No water after five o'clock. She said I might wet the bed. I told her I haven't wet the bed since I was six, but she still wouldn't let me have anything after five. And she made me go to bed at eight. I felt like a baby."

That didn't sit well with me, either, but I kept that to myself. I made a mental note to talk to Tara about that. "Dinner's almost ready," I said, wanting to get things going. "Why don't you go put your things in your room and wash up? When you come back down I'll have everything ready."

"Okay." He picked up the bag he'd left on the floor by the door. "I just wish Mom would've taken the news better. I wanted her and Rebel to get along. They talked nice to each other when I introduced them."

"Give her time, Little Buddy. Your mom just needs to get used to things." I put my arm around his shoulders and ushered him out of the kitchen.

With Eli gone, Rebel came back in. "So, what's up?"

Ladling the chili into three bowls, I filled her in. "He told his mother about you and me. Tara cried."

Rebel deflated and took a seat on the barstool Eli had just vacated. "Damn."

"Yeah." Pulling the cornbread out of the oven, I put the pan on the stovetop then went to get the butter from the fridge. "He nearly broke my heart, telling me how sad he was about her crying."

"I bet." Rebel's eyes were fixed on the spot in front of her. I knew she was probably trying to think of a way to make everything better.

"Rebel, it's going to take time is all." I knew that was the only thing that would help. "I just don't understand. *She* left. She was dating before we ever even filed for divorce. Did she think I would just sit around and do nothing while she moved on with her life?"

"I guess so," Rebel mumbled.

"Eli told me that Tara said something about her thinking we'd be a family again one day." That comment threw me for a loop. She'd never mentioned a thing like that to me. "It kind of pisses me off that she thinks she can do whatever she wants, then come back home when she's done."

Rebel nodded. "I can understand why that makes you mad." She looked up, and my eyes caught the glistening of what looked like tears in hers. "So, what are we going to do about this?"

"Nothing." I knew Tara didn't want to come back home. I knew she wasn't anywhere near done with sowing her wilds oats. She'd only taken Eli because another woman had made her feel guilty about not seeing him. "If I let her back in, then she'll only stay for a short time. I know that. I don't want her back, anyway."

Gulping, I saw the lump go down Rebel's throat. "What makes you so sure of that?"

"We never loved each other, Rebel." I picked up our bowls and placed them on the table.

"But you lived together for about six years without love. I'm sure she thinks you could just go back to that." Rebel picked up the buttered cornbread and brought it to the table.

Turning, I looked at her. "I can't go back to that life. I might've been able to before, but I can't now."

"Because of me?" she asked, her gaze penetrating.

"Yes." Taking her by the shoulders, I kissed her on the forehead. "My feelings for you are already so much stronger than anything I've ever felt for her. How can I throw that all away?"

Rebel took in a sharp breath. "What if she wants to stay with you because of Eli? What if sharing her kid as well as her ex is just too much for her?"

"Too bad." I sat down at the table, not the least bit hungry anymore. Then I looked at Rebel, watching as she chewed her lower lip nervously. "Why are you looking like that?"

Shaking her head, she put her finger to her lips as Eli came back in. "You hungry, Eli?"

"Chili's one of my favorites." He sat down and dug right in.

Rebel sat down, too. She and I picked at our food, neither of us having much of an appetite any longer. I could see it in her eyes that she thought I might let Tara back if she wanted to come home.

But I'd found something better with Rebel. "After dinner, Rebel and I have a surprise for you, Eli. We've been as busy as elves this weekend." Maybe if Rebel heard me making plans for our future then she'd realize I had no intention of letting her go—not for anyone.

"Really?" Eli's eyes shined brightly as he looked at Rebel. "What did you guys do?"

Finally, the light came back to her eyes. "Something for you."

After dinner, we took Eli to where we'd set up the tree. When he saw three presents under it with his name on them, he jumped up and down with excitement. "Yeah! Three presents already."

"You'll never guess what they are." Rebel had hunted for the most unique presents she could find for Eli. She was right—he'd never guess that a pet rock was one of his gifts. Especially since she'd put it in a huge box.

Everyone wore smiles again, and the sadness over Tara's reaction seemed to be pushed back. For a while, anyway.

18

REBEL

LOOKING at my cell while the vet tech pulled out the rotten tooth of an old Golden Retriever, I saw Harman's name flash on the screen. We should have been closed an hour earlier, but when Mrs. Nelson had called about her desperate dog, I said I'd stay open until she got there. "Do you have this, Jimmy?"

He nodded. "Yeah. He's not even bleeding because that tooth was so decayed. I'll clean him all up, then put him in a cage to sleep off the anesthesia."

"I'll stay until you're all done here. I've gotta lock up after." I swiped the screen to answer the call then walked out of the exam room. "Hi, handsome."

"Hey, gorgeous." I heard him sigh. "I just passed your house and you're not home. Where might you be?"

"Still at the clinic." I sat down in one of the chairs in the lobby. "We had a late emergency. I'll be leaving in just a bit."

"Come to my place for dinner. Rene is making roast goose," he told me.

"I'll be there. See you soon." I ended the call and looked up to see a car pulling up in front of the glass doors. I'd locked them, so I took out my keys and opened them back up to tell the person that we were closed.

When Tara got out of the car, I felt as if the wind had been knocked out of me. "Can we talk?" She came toward me.

Stepping back, I let her inside, then locked the doors again. "This must be pretty important for you to come to my place of work, Tara."

"I saw your car as I was driving by and decided it had to be a sign." She looked around the lobby. "Is anyone else here?"

"Jimmy's in the back. Once he's done, I'll need to lock up." I crossed my arms in front of me. "So what would you like to talk about?" I was not at all comfortable with her being in my clinic, but I didn't want to be rude to Eli's mother.

Shifting her weight back and forth, she seemed agitated. "I feel like you're getting in the way of things, Rebel."

"How's that?" I did not like where this conversation was headed and found it pretty presumptuous of her to think she could dictate what anyone else did with their personal lives. She'd left Harman. What more was there to say?

"Eli talks about you all the time. Even more than he talks about his father." She began tapping her long, manicured nails on top of the front desk. "I don't like it. He's *our* son, Rebel. *Ours.*" She looked me in the eye to make her point.

"I know whose kid he is, Tara. I'm not trying to take anyone's place. And I'm not trying to get in the way your relationship with your son." She had no idea how much I would love to see her spending more time with Eli. "Tara, you can have that boy as much as you want. You're the one who keeps preventing that from happening, not me."

"He's so busy with you all the time," she said, throwing her hands in the air and starting to pace. "He's always messing with your animals. He's always with *you.*"

"And his father is there, too." I wasn't sure if that was helping or hurting my side of things. "Eli can be with you as much as you want him—Harman's told me that on many occasions. It's up to you, not the stupid court documents, and Harman would never stop you either. You can have Eli as much as you want."

Stopping in her tracks, she looked at me. "I shouldn't have to compete with you for my son's attention."

"There's no competition, Tara. You're his mother. End of story." I couldn't believe she felt threatened by me. "I want that boy to have a great relationship with you. Everyone wants that, Tara. No one is standing in your way."

"But *you* are. I don't see how you can't realize that." Her eyes pleaded with me. "Step back. Give me room. Please."

"I can try to give you room, but you're seeing something that's not there." I threw my hands in the air in exasperation. "You've stepped back from spending time with your kid, and now you want me to do the same thing to the poor boy? Why? Why do you seem to think that having only Harman in his life is best for Eli? That's what you left it at before, and you were fine with that."

"His father's always been is his hero," she said. "Now it sounds like you've taken over that role. And now Eli loves you, so of course Harman loves you, too."

That gave me pause. Did Harman only care for me because I'd won over Eli? It was too much to think about just then.

"Of course Eli looks up to his father. They have a wonderful relationship. And you could have that, too. No one is standing in your way but you, Tara. You're making excuses." I took a seat, feeling exasperated, but not wanting the woman to feel threatened by me. "Let's sit and talk."

She sat a few chairs over. "You have no idea what it's like to have your life end at only nineteen."

"That's how you see it?" I asked with astonishment. "You feel like your life ended when you got pregnant?"

"It did." A tear fell down her cheek. "I didn't even know Harman when I got pregnant."

"Yeah, he told me the whole sordid tale." It had shocked me that Harman had ever been the kind of man who'd have sex in a dirty bar restroom with a woman he'd never met before.

"Okay, so you know how much older he was than me. He was like a grown man already. And I was still a kid." Another tear fell down her cheek. "Can you put yourself in my shoes for a minute?"

"Tell me, Tara." I wanted to understand her, I really did.

She wiped the tears away with the back of her hand, smudging her makeup. "My father made me marry Harman. Harman didn't blink an eye when my father told him that he would get a DNA test done, and if the baby was his, he expected Harman to do the right thing and marry me. I stood there like a side of beef being sold. It was humiliating."

"I agree. That must've been a horrible time for you." My heart ached for her. But it ached for Harman, too. "But it happened. And it wasn't all bad, now was it? Harman's a nice man. He isn't mean or hateful."

"No, he's nice. At least I got lucky there." She looked up at the ceiling. "But I wasn't attracted to him—not in the way you should be when you marry someone. I was so young and ignorant, and he just seemed so old to me then. And when we went to his apartment after getting married, he didn't make me have sex with him, but he didn't make me *want* to have sex with him, either. And that just set the tone for everything. It was so...disconnected."

"It was mechanical," I said. Harman had described it that way to me when he told me the story.

"Yes. And it felt like that act cemented the fact that I now belonged to him. And that killed me inside." She sobbed, and I got up to hug her.

"I'm so sorry you went through that. And at such a young age, too. If you had been older, you would've realized you two didn't have to get married to raise your baby together." The answer to all this was an easy one, even though it wouldn't be a quick fix. "Tara, you need therapy. What you've gone through would get to anyone."

She put her hands against me, pushing me away. "You doctors are always throwing more doctors at people. There's no one who can fix what's happened to me. No amount of talking will change things. Why do any of you think that it will?"

The woman was as confused as she was wrong. "Tara, talking to someone who's educated about your situation does help. I promise you, it does. Besides, plenty of people who aren't doctors—of the human or animal variety—would recommend the same thing."

She looked into my eyes as her lower lip quivered. "Harman took me, and he married me without asking me if that's what I wanted. Nobody ever asked what *I* wanted."

"He was hurt by the forced marriage, too, Tara. Don't think he wasn't." I didn't understand everything about their unique situation, but I knew that much. "He knew you didn't love him, but he married you anyway. He did everything for you, and once your son came, he did everything for both of you. He did everything he knew how to do to be a good husband and father. And it is tragic that neither of you understood how to make things right between you and that your communication was so terrible that you couldn't be honest with one another. But he never meant to hurt you. He never meant to scar you."

"I know." She broke down again, and I hugged her once more. "I did grow to love him. I think...I think it was love. I don't know for sure. But I grew to respect Harman. And Eli respects him, too. And now Eli respects you. And I'm the only one without an ounce of respect coming my way."

At that point, she wasn't doing a thing to deserve it. But I didn't want to put it that way. "If you want respect, you have to earn it. Just giving respect to others doesn't automatically make them respect you. Eli loves you. If you start doing right by him, if you listen to him and work at being a part of his life, then you will earn his respect. In the process, you'll earn Harman's, too. He desperately wants you in Eli's life, Tara."

"I feel like I can't be in Eli's life if you are." She looked at me with drooping eyes. "I never expected Harman to move on—it's been two years and he hasn't tried until now. And I thought if he ever did, that he for sure wouldn't allow another woman around our son."

"I'm sorry, but I don't know why you would have come to expect that," I let her know. "Life does go on, Tara."

"I thought I'd get out there and live life a bit, and that I could go back as soon as I'd done all the things I'd missed out on by ruining my life and getting pregnant." She shifted in her seat. "And I think I've done all that. I'm ready for my old life again. But I can't have it back if you're standing in my way, Rebel. Woman to woman, please— I want my family back."

I sat there, my stomach aching, my heart pounding, and my mind telling me that this is what Harman had meant when he said he'd take Tara back if it meant Eli could have a normal family again.

And I had no idea what I was supposed to do.

19

HARMAN

I WAS WAITING for Rebel to show up at my house, and when my cell rang instead, I answered it with a wariness I'd never felt with Rebel before. "What's up, baby? Where are you?"

"At my place." She hesitated, making my heart race. "Can you come over here to talk after you put Eli to bed?"

"You don't want to come over?" I'd had the chef keep dinner warm, so we could all eat together.

"No," came her reply. "I'll tell you about it when you come over later."

Something told me that things weren't right. "Okay, I'll see you a bit after nine."

Eli and I ate dinner in a confused silence. "So, Rebel just didn't want to come eat dinner with us?" Eli asked after a few minutes of quiet.

"I guess that emergency at the clinic didn't end well." That's all I could think. *What else could it be?*

"Yeah, maybe someone's pet died, and it made Rebel too sad to eat." He stabbed a piece of roast goose. "Don't tell Miss Rene, but I'm not a fan of this dinner."

"She did her best." I was sure the goose was well-received by most of the upper-crust types she'd served in her career. "And you and I don't have the palate most of her clients do."

"I don't know what that means," he said as he rolled his eyes. "But I think I like hot dogs more than I like this."

"Precisely." I smiled as I watched him take a bite of roasted red potato.

Later, after our nightly swim, I tucked Eli into bed and went to tell the maid she could leave after I got back. Then I got into my Maserati and went to see Rebel.

The door was locked when I got there, and I had to ring the bell. She was expecting me, so I wondered why she'd locked the door. When she answered it wearing a robe, she didn't say a word, just stepped back to let me inside.

Her demeanor wasn't exactly cold, but it was different. Far different than it had been just hours earlier. "No kiss?" She shook her head, and I knew then that something was definitely wrong. "Did you catch a cold or something?"

She pointed to the sofa. "Sit, please."

"Okay." I took a seat and Rebel sat on the chair opposite me. "Just spit it out, baby. Whatever it is, we can work through it."

"I'm not sure you'd even want to." She looked up at the ceiling, and I saw the sheen of tears in her eyes. She shook her head, willing them away before looking back at me. "Tara stopped by the clinic to see me."

That sounded bad. "Why?"

"She said that she hadn't planned on doing it. But she saw my car there and thought it was an omen." Rebel looked at me then, and a tear fell down her cheek. "She's a very damaged woman, Harman. I'm not saying it's your fault, because that's not entirely the truth. But she's damaged."

"I agree." I'd always known our pregnancy had hurt Tara a hell of a lot. "But she refuses therapy. So what can I do?"

She shrugged her narrow shoulders, and I knew she didn't have a solution this time. "All I know is that I threaten her."

"I can see that." On the surface, Tara had every reason to feel threatened. But that was only because she didn't realize that Rebel only wanted what was best for Eli—and that meant a relationship between Tara and Eli.

"Do you remember what you told me when we first met? About if Tara ever wanted to come back and try to put your family back together?" she asked. I felt my heart filling with dread.

"Has she told you she wants that?" I didn't care if she did or not. I didn't love Tara—never had. But I loved Eli with everything I had in me, and that made things difficult.

Nodding, she confirmed my suspicions. "And I told her I would step out of her way."

What did she say? "You did what?"

"She told me I was standing in the way of your family getting back together." Another tear rolled down her cheek. "And she's right. I can't give you what she can. I can't give Eli his family back—and that's what you really want. You told me so when we first met."

"Baby, no. I see another way to live now, one that I hadn't realized before." I got up, feeling the need to pace. I could feel what Rebel and I had slipping away from me. "Don't let her do this to us, Rebel. I can't believe you would tell her that you'd get out of her way. This is the first relationship I've had, and she's probably just freaked out. She'll grow to understand things."

"It hasn't been that long since you told me you wanted her back in your home if she wanted to be there." More tears fell, and my heart ached worse with each one I witnessed.

"Don't cry, baby." I went to hold her and hug her, to tell her everything would be alright.

But her hands met my chest, stopping me. "Please don't, Harman. This is so hard for me, as it is. If you touch me, hold me, kiss me, I won't be able to do what I need to do for Eli and you."

"I don't want her back, Rebel," I told her. "Doesn't that mean anything to you? She can be in Eli's life, but she doesn't have to be in mine. Not like that. I've never loved anyone until you."

Her eyes shimmered as she looked into mine. "You love me?"

"I do." It had to be love. My heart had never ached like this over anyone. Not even when Tara had left me. "If you think you're leaving me so that she can try to win me over, then don't. She can't."

"I told her I'd give her room to try. I didn't say I'd end it all, but I think that would be best." She shook her head. "She's right, Harman. I'm not doing you or Eli any favors by getting involved in all this. If I'd never butted in with Eli and Tara, we probably wouldn't even be here anyway. I didn't mean to use him to get to you, but you only even started paying attention to me because of how I am with your son.

"What?" That had me genuinely confused. "None of that is true." I adored how she was with Eli, but that wasn't everything I loved about her. And I knew she'd started caring about him way before she ever started caring about me. If she thought she'd used my affection for Eli to get noticed, then I could say I was guilty of the same. "You and I share a connection I've never felt with anyone else. That doesn't have anything to do with Tara, and it doesn't have anything to do with Eli, either. I never loved Tara, and she never loved me. There's nothing else to say to that."

"But what if she did love you?" Rebel looked away from me. "Sometimes it takes someone else having what you took for granted to realize everything you had but didn't appreciate. I think she's found something to love in you now. Now that she's older and feels like she can make her own choices. And you've always wanted that, until I came along."

"Only because I was ready to settle. I didn't know what love felt like." In everything that Rebel had said, she never once said that she didn't love Eli and me. "And now you know what love feels like, too. So how can you walk away and leave that? Leave us?"

She ignored my question. "Tara is Eli's mother, and she's your wife—separated only by a divorce paper." She pulled a tissue out of the pocket of her robe.

"You say *divorce paper* like it's nothing!" It felt like she just kept coming up with excuses. Instead of fighting *for* me, it felt like she was fighting *against* me. And I couldn't keep fighting for both of us. "If you're going to put it that way, the only thing that made her my wife was a couple of papers. She was never my wife in my heart, no matter how much I tried to make that work. You have to believe that."

I went to my knees in front of her. "I love you. I know I've beaten around the bush about it, but I love you. And I don't want to lose you. I'll never want her again, Rebel. I know I won't. Not when I know what love feels like with you. Even if you step back, I won't take her back."

She looked at me with watery eyes. "But Harman, what if you can have the family you always wanted? You should give it a chance. And for the record, I love you, too. I'm doing this *because* I love you—you and Eli. He's the most important person in all this. You and I both know that. He deserves to have his mother and father raise him together, the way things like that are meant to be."

"I'll admit that I've always thought that." But now things were different. "But I don't think that way anymore. I never thought another woman could bond with my son the way he'd need. I thought that only his biological mother could love him unconditionally. I was wrong. You love him as much as any mother could. You treat him like he's yours already."

"And that's why you love me, Harman." She stroked my hair. "If I were dismissive with Eli, then you wouldn't have given me the time of day."

"You're right." Eli was the center of my world, after all. "I wouldn't have hit it off with you if you showed no interest in my son, but I'm not in love with you because you did. And you didn't use him to get to me. You probably could've tried, if you'd been a different kind of person. That's exactly what Tara is trying to do—use him to get what she wants. And you're going to tell me that you love Eli and me, but that you'll step back and let another woman take us from you?"

"I took you away from her first." Her lower lip quivered. "I know she hasn't been around. And I won't stand back if she refuses to step forward. But if she steps up...it's in your best interest to do what's best for you and your son. "

Now I was feeling frustrated—and a little desperate. I knew there was only one woman for me. And I knew there was room in Eli's life for more than one. "That boy has room in his heart for all of us. You know that."

"His mother doesn't." Rebel wasn't budging.

If I knew anything about the woman I'd fallen in love with, it was that when she felt something was right, there wasn't a thing anyone could do to make her think differently. I just had to make her see that the right thing here was for her to be with me and Eli. We both needed her. "I tell you what, if Tara steps up, then we'll see how things go between her and Eli. And I won't pressure you to see my son or me in the meantime. But if you see that she's not stepping into the opening you give her, then can you promise me you'll put this behind us?"

She looked at me for a heart-pounding moment before she let out a huge sigh. "I love you." She put her hands on either side of my face. "And I want to be with you. I don't want things to change at all. But I feel she has the right to have one more shot at the family you two made together. If she doesn't do what's right, I won't stand back any longer. But if she does, then I will fade into the woodwork, and you and Eli won't have to see me again. That's a promise."

As if either of us would ever stand for that. The thought of never seeing Rebel Saxe again filled me with a mix of emotions that startled me. Rage being chief among them.

20

REBEL

WATCHING Harman leave my home nearly killed me. When I got home the next day to find Eli in my backyard taking care of the animals, I knew Harman hadn't told him a thing.

"Hi, Rebel," he said as I walked out the back door. "I heard you pull up. Were you feeling bad yesterday? Is that why you didn't come eat that roast goose with us? Or was it 'cause you hate roast goose? 'Cause I didn't know that I hated it, but I do. And Dad hates it, too. So I understand if you didn't want to come eat that yucky food."

"Um," I didn't know how to phrase what I needed to tell him. It was clear his father hadn't prepared him at all. "Well, let's start with this. Have you heard from your mother today?"

When he shook his head, my jaw dropped. She should've called him, at the very least. "Why?"

"Well, your mom stopped by my work yesterday, and we had a talk." I took his hand, leading him inside. "Let's get some hot chocolate and warm up a little." It was chilly out, and I thought a treat might ease the harshness of what I had to say. "I'll make it with almond milk, so it won't hurt your tummy."

"Thanks." He smiled at me as he ran his hand in a circle over his tummy. "The squirty poops hurt my stomach."

"I know." Taking him inside, I felt the same rock in my gut that I had when Harman had been over the night before. "Take a seat, and I'll make the drinks."

Sitting at the table, he looked at me and asked, "So, what did Mom say to you?"

"She told me that she wants to be in your life a lot more." His eyes lit up at my words, and that made me happy. Like this wouldn't all be in vain.

"Good," he said. "I want her more in my life."

After spending the day feeling awful about how everything had went with Harman, this conversation with Eli was already turning into just the reminder I needed of why I'd decided to step back. The boy needed his mother in his life more than he needed me. After heating the almond milk, I filled two mugs then stirred in chocolate syrup. Plopping a couple of mini marshmallows on top of his, I put the cups on the table then took a seat. "Here ya go, Eli."

"Thanks." He blew the steam off the top. "Looks good."

"Thanks." I sipped mine, then decided to just get straight to the point. "Since your mom wants to spend more time with you, I want to make sure that you know you can go with her or spend time with her if she's at your house. You know, you can leave the animals to me. I can take care of them on my own. I don't want you missing out on spending time with your mom."

"That's nice of you, Rebel." He patted the back of my hand, which rested on the table. "I know you want my mom to be a good mom. She wouldn't have taken me last weekend if you hadn't talked to her on the phone. You're a good influence on her, you know?"

"You think I'm a good influence on her?" I smiled at that. "Perhaps I am." If nothing else, I'd shown her that both Eli and Harman were wonderful people that others—at least me—liked to be around.

"You are." After taking a sip, he added, "And she's even caring about Dad more. That makes me happy, too. She hasn't cared about him." He looked up as if trying to think of a time when she had. "Never. Yeah, she's never cared about him."

"What makes you think that, Eli?" I knew she couldn't have been that uncaring toward Harman, a man who was once her husband.

"Dad was really sick this one time. I was in kindergarten, and he couldn't get out of bed." He took another sip. "This is so good, Rebel. You should put this recipe in a contest or something, 'cause you'd win."

"Thank you." I took another sip. "It is good, isn't it? Go on with what you were saying, Eli."

"Oh, yeah. Dad was in bed and throwing up real bad. I felt so bad for him and even told Mom that I could stay home to take care of him." He looked at the cookies on the counter. "Can I have one of those?"

Getting up, I brought the plate to the table. "Sure, Slugger."

"So anyway, Mom just laughed and said he was a grown man and he'd be fine on his own. She needed to get me to school, and she had some things to do." He took the cookie I handed him. "Thank you, Rebel. I felt bad for Dad. And when we got home after school, he was still in bed. He asked me to hand him his cell phone, so he could call Nana 'cause he needed help."

Even though my stomach knotted at the story, I told myself that Tara had been young and inexperienced. "Well, I'm sure your mom just didn't know what to do." When I thought about it, Tara had likely been around twenty-five at the time that had taken place—my age. I couldn't imagine leaving a sick and miserable Harman to fend for himself.

"Yeah, she's not very much like most moms." My doorbell rang, and he looked over his shoulder. "That's probably Dad."

"Oh?" It felt weird having Harman ring the doorbell like any other guest in my home. But it was a necessity if I was going to put space between us.

I went to the door and opened it to find Harman standing there with a grim expression. "It's cold. I thought I should come pick Eli up. So he doesn't have to walk in the cold."

He should've known I would take the kid home. "Come in."

Moving awkwardly, he stepped inside. "You ready to go, Eli?"

Eli's eyes scanned us. "Why aren't you two giving each other hugs and kisses?"

Harman looked at me out of the corner of his eye. "Rebel hasn't told you about your mother, Eli?"

"Not that part." I didn't know how to talk to the boy about something so adult.

"What about what Mom told you, Rebel?" Eli got up and came to the living room. The three of us stood there in a semi-circle, Eli and Harman wearing near-identical frowns. "I want to know why you and Dad aren't acting right."

Harman looked to me to answer that. I had no choice. "So, your mom wants to spend more time with you and your dad. And she'd like it if I didn't do as much with you two—so she can do things with you guys. Like a real family. I'm not your family, Eli."

Eli took my hand. "Rebel, don't make me stop coming over 'cause of my mom. Please." His pleading voice always got to me and denying him now was more difficult than ever before. "She won't come around. You'll see. She's got other things to do."

"I know she's *had* other things to do." I looked a Harman, and all I got was a frown from him. "But she said she's going to put you guys first. And I need to respect that."

Holding on to my leg, Eli looked up at me with pleading eyes now, too. "If she comes to get me or comes over to visit us, then I won't come here. But if she's not coming around, then please let me come over. I love the animals, and I love you, Rebel."

There was a catch in Eli's voice that broke my heart. I stared down at this boy who I'd come to care for so much, at a loss for words. Harman cleared his throat, breaking the momentary silence. "So do I."

Eli looked at his dad, a more hopeful look on his face. "See, we both love you. Don't make us leave you alone."

The way they looked at me made me feel as if I'd made a horrible decision. But when the two guys you love the most in the world have a chance at ultimate happiness, what's a woman supposed to do? "Okay. If she doesn't follow through with what she said she would, then things don't have to change." I looked at Harman, who finally had a smile on his face. I'd missed his smile. "But as far as dating goes, we should still chill on that, Harman," I said in a quieter voice.

"I don't think so," he said, reaching out to take my hands as Eli clung to my leg. "We love you."

"And I love you both, too." I ran my hand over Eli's head as I looked into Harman's eyes. "I love you both so much that I would put what *I* want to the side to make sure you both have everything you want and need."

"We need *you*," Eli wailed.

And now I felt like *I* was hurting them. I never wanted to hurt anyone. But no matter what I did, someone would be hurting.

Tara had said she thought she'd found love for Harman. Maybe he didn't know that. Maybe he needed to know that—and not hear it from me. "Just promise me you'll give her a chance if she comes to you guys."

"If you promise you won't go nowhere, we will," Eli said.

I didn't know if that was a promise I could make. If they welcome Tara back into their lives, I didn't know if I could be around that— seeing all the love that I wished could be mine. And Harman knew I wouldn't tell either of them a lie. "Little Buddy, if Rebel feels like she needs to give your mother a chance, then we need to let her do what she feels is right."

I nodded. "Thank you, Harman."

The grim expression had returned. "Even if we think she's silly for what she's doing, we have to allow Rebel to do what she feels is right in her heart. We have to do that because when you love someone, you let them do what they feel they have to do. Even if it hurts."

"But I don't ever want to lose you, Rebel," Eli whimpered.

Running my hand over his head, I had no idea what the right thing to do was anymore. My boys were hurting, and I hated that more than I had ever hated anything.

But giving them false promises felt wrong. So I told them the only thing I could. "For now, things will stay the same." Only they wouldn't be the same. I'd make sure to stay busy at work, leaving time for Tara to step in and take over the role that had always been hers.

Harman took me into his arms. "This is the right thing to do, baby. Don't leave us just because you think she'll do what's right. Even if she does, I'll still want you in my life."

"Me, too," Eli echoed. "Please, Rebel, never leave us."

I'd known it would be hard for me to take a step back, but I hadn't realized just how much Eli and Harman would be affected by my choices. I knew they'd be upset, but I hadn't known the depth of their need for me. And now that I knew their feelings matched my own, I didn't know how I could stand back to see what Tara would do to these guys who held my heart.

Was I hurting them just so that Tara could swoop in and hurt them all over again? She hadn't ever taken care of either of them when she had the chance, so why let her have them now? Why let her neglect them any further? They didn't deserve that.

And neither did I.

21

HARMAN

WHEN THREE DAYS passed with no added effort from Tara—she still made her daily phone calls to Eli, but nothing more—I thought she'd had enough time to show whether she meant to follow through on what she'd told Rebel. Just as I'd thought, she really didn't want more time with either of us. Tara just didn't want anyone else in the picture.

Well, this was one thing that Tara wasn't going to get her way on.

Even though Rebel had found things to keep her busy into the evenings, Eli and I still managed to spend an hour or so with her each day. Neither of us wanted Rebel to slip through our fingers. And I knew Rebel didn't want that either. It was evident in the bright smile she couldn't keep off her face when she saw us coming through her door.

I planned to give it until the end of the week. If Tara hadn't stepped up before that, then I was going to be the one to put my ex in her place. I was the one Tara should have come to in the first place, not Rebel. Eli and I weren't her playthings to be kept on a shelf until she was ready to give us her attention.

Eli and I rode home after I'd picked him up from school. I had no patients in the hospital to see, so I took off early to get him. When his cell rang, I listened in as he answered. "Hi, Mom."

He'd put the phone on speaker and laid it in his lap, so I heard Tara reply, "Hi, Eli. What're your plans for today?"

"Why?" he asked as he looked at me with surprise. "You coming to pick me up?"

"Oh, not today," she said quickly. "I've got a shipment coming in. I've got to be here. Maybe next week I can get you. If your father lets me."

Eli looked at me and I nodded. "He would let you get me."

"I'll have to talk to him and see," Tara said. "What have you guys been up to these last few days, Eli? Still feeding Rebel's animals for her?"

"Yes," he said.

It didn't take a millisecond for Tara's voice to turn shrill. "What? Didn't she tell you that she didn't need your help any longer?"

Eli looked out the window with a frown on his face. "She did tell me that. But I begged her to let me keep helping. I love those animals, and I love helping. And I love her, too, Mom!"

"That bitch!" she shouted.

I pulled to the side of the road and picked up the phone, turning it off speaker. "Look, I don't want you talking to Eli like that."

"So, you're listening in on our private conversations now?" Tara asked, sounding hostile. "She and I had an agreement. I guess she didn't tell you or Eli about it."

"You and I need to talk." I was done with her trying to run the show. "I'll meet you at that café down the street from your shop. I'm sure you can find the time to walk two doors over."

"I can't," she said.

I wasn't taking no for an answer. "You can and you will. I'm dropping Eli off at home, then heading that way. This ends today, Tara."

"No!" was all she got out before I ended the call and put the cell in my pocket.

"For a little while, until I straighten things out, I'd rather you not talk to your mom, Little Buddy. She's a bit mixed up right now."

"She sure is." He looked at me with furrowed brows. "Why'd she call Rebel that bad word?"

I knew why. But my kid didn't need to be worried about the issues the adults in his life were dealing with. "She's just got to get used to things is all. I'll talk to her. We'll work this out. You'll see." I wasn't sure what we would work out. But I knew something had to be done.

An hour later, I sat in the café waiting for Tara to arrive. Finally, she strolled in with one of her young employees at her side. For emotional support, I guessed. "Hi, Harman. This is Rachel. She's in the mood for a mocha latte, and I told her she could come along with me."

I didn't bother with niceties, "Rachel, my ex-wife and I have something important to discuss, and this meeting was intended to be private. So you'll have to forgive my rudeness, but you're not invited to sit in on this."

Ducking her head, she whispered, "Whoa, I'm outie." Then she went right back out the door.

Tara looked stunned as she watched her friend go. "Um, you don't have to leave..."

"Yes, she does." I got up and took Tara by the arm, leading her to the booth bench across from where I'd been sitting. "We've got lots to talk about."

The waitress came over to the table. "What can I get you?" she asked Tara.

"Nothing." Tara looked up at her. "I won't be staying long."

With a nod, the waitress left us, as I already had a cup of coffee in front of me. Finally alone, I got the ball rolling. "Rebel told me what you asked her to do. And I think it's the most selfish thing you've ever done. You've paid very little attention to your son. Rebel is the first person to give him some, and you're asking us to shut her out."

Her green eyes sparkled with anger as she ran a hand through her red hair. "She's taking more than she has any right to."

"That's not true at all." I could see the jealousy radiating through my ex-wife, and it was time we got to the real issue. "You're jealous."

"Of what?" She laughed as if that was ridiculous. "I'm his mother." Her eyes narrowed at me. "*You* and *I* are his parents, Harman. She's nothing to either of you. *I'm* his mother, and I'm the mother of *your* only child. That makes *me* more important to both of you than *she* should ever be. But you two seem to have forgotten that, haven't you? I only asked her to do what was right—to step back and let me have my family back."

"You never even wanted us." I laid it out there for her. "As soon as I had money, you saw your way out and took it. And you've never looked back. Not until we found someone else."

"It's not right." Her hands twisted on top of the table. "Harman, I've never been so lonely."

"You spoke to Rebel three days ago. You've had three days to spend time with your son, and you haven't spent one minute with him." I took a drink of my coffee to steady myself as anger filled me. "And what's this crap about wanting me back, Tara. You haven't mentioned anything like to me—ever. You never wanted me in the first place. I still try to wrap my head around why the hell you even pulled me into that bathroom that night."

"I wish I understood that myself, Harman." She eyed me warily. "I really do. But I did it and I can't take it back. Why can't I make the most of it now? I can see things in you now that were never there before. Your smile is different now, and you have this glow about you. And it's attractive. I'm only human. And you *were* mine. And I am the mother of your son. We share a connection you don't have with her."

"And she and I share a connection I've never shared with you," I let her know.

The grimace on her face told me I'd hurt her. "Well, what you and I share is more important. We love our son, and we'd do anything for him—including putting love behind us to do what's right for him. We did that for years; why can't we go back to that?"

She was right—that's exactly what we'd done for so many years. We'd forgone love or even *like* to get married and provide a family for the baby we'd made. No matter how he'd come about, Eli was the glue that had always kept us together. "You left, Tara."

"I know I did." She looked at me with tears in her eyes. "Harman, I was a kid when I had Eli. I needed some time to live—to find out what I'd been missing. But I'm done with that now. It turns out I hadn't been missing much. I just want to get back to being the family we were before."

"So, you had your fun, and it wasn't as fun as you wanted it to be, so now you think I should just let you move back in?" I asked with bewilderment. "Into my home—and my bed, too?"

"I know you don't want me in your bed. Not yet." She looked off to one side. "Maybe not ever, now that you've had her. But I want the chance to show you that I can make you happy. Let me be the wife and mother I was before things went wrong."

She hadn't been that good at either of those things before. Why would I give her a chance to go back to that when I could have so much more?

Because she's Eli's mother.

I didn't know what the right answer was anymore. If I had never met Rebel, I might have taken Tara back right there. But that doesn't mean it would've been the right thing to do. "Why don't we start with you being the mother you need to be to your son, Tara?"

Her jaw set with that look that said she wanted things her way— and her way only. "Harman, you told me over and over again that I could come back home whenever I wanted to. And now that I'm telling you I want to come home, you won't let me."

"You waited too long." I picked up my coffee and took another drink. "And you haven't done half of what you should've been doing in the meantime."

"I can't be what you want me to be for Eli if I can't live with him— and you." She shook her head as she went on, "I don't know how to parent without you, Harman. That's why I haven't taken Eli much. And having him at my place feels wrong."

"You've always had the opportunity to come to my place to spend time with him," I reminded her. "You chose not to."

Pushing her hand through her hair, she said, "You can't imagine how hard it was to be around you, Harman. You looked at me as if I'd ruined your life by leaving. And you thought I'd be able to be myself with you around? You're crazy."

I thought she was the one who was acting crazy. "Tara, what do you want? Do you want me to drop the woman I love so that I can be your lackluster husband again?"

When she nodded, I almost fell out of my chair. "Why not?"

She hadn't found what I had, so how could I blame her for asking such an insane thing? "Look, Tara, it might have taken me a long time to realize it, but you were right to leave me. What we had together was a hardly a life. I had no idea what I'd been missing, either. But then Rebel moved in, and I found it. And I'm not giving it up for you. Sorry, but I can't do that."

Tara's hands clenched tightly into fists. "She promised me she'd step back. She lied."

"She has stepped back as much as we'd let her." I'd been so relieved when Eli had fought just as hard against Rebel's ridiculous concession to Tara's request as I had. "Eli and I both love Rebel. And she loves us so much that she was willing to be selfless when she thought that she was standing in the way of our happiness. She made space—space she never needed to give in the first place—and you didn't fill it."

"She didn't give me enough time." Tara shook her head. "She didn't do what she said she would. You two are still around her every day. How am I supposed to compete with her? She's got a career like yours. She's got these animals that Eli adores. And what do I have? A boutique that neither of you cares about."

"But we do care about *you*, Tara." I may not have loved the woman, but she was the mother of my son, and I would always have a place in my heart for her. "I want things to work out for all of us. I want you to feel comfortable in my home. I want you to feel comfortable around Rebel."

Shaking her head, she let me know, "That's never going to happen, Harman. She has to go if you want me to stay."

22

REBEL

WITH NOTHING else to do at work, the clinic director told me to go home and chill out a bit. She said it seemed like I had a lot on my mind, and she'd been right. I hadn't realized how much it showed. So, on my way home, I stopped by the liquor store to get a bottle of Jack and some soda to mix it with.

Come hell or high water I was going to chill out.

Sipping on a relatively concentrated drink, I sat on my sofa and read a historical romance that promised me lots of steamy action. As I relaxed into the couch, I let the warmth of the fireplace lull me into a sense of security—even when I felt the most insecure I'd ever felt in my entire life.

I hadn't left the door as open as I'd promised Tara I would, and I knew there would have to be a confrontation about that sometime. With no idea when or how that would occur, I'd been walking around on pins and needles for the last few days.

And then there was the idea that I would soon lose Harman and Eli. That didn't feel good either. Not much felt good at this point. But sipping on the alcoholic beverage while basking in the glow of the fireplace—now that felt awesome.

The sound of a car driving slowly by had me looking up from my book and out the front window. And there I saw Tara's car creeping by my house. My stomach knotted, knowing she was on her way to Harman's.

As much as I wanted her in Eli's life, I didn't want her in Harman's. I knew that was selfish of me, but I couldn't help it. It wouldn't stop me from keeping my distance though, not if that was what was best for Eli.

Thinking that a bit more Jack in my Coke would help me get through this initial Tara visit, I got up and filled the empty space in my tall glass with pure alcohol. Giving it a stir, I took a sip and coughed.

When my front door swung open to show a figure standing in the doorway with snow flurrying around broad shoulders, I almost cried with relief. "Harman!"

"Hey, gorgeous." He moved with graceful speed, taking me into his arms.

I'd abandoned my drink, leaving it on the counter in the kitchen. "I didn't think you'd be coming over tonight. I thought I saw her drive by."

His kissed me, putting an end to my words. Moving my hands along his strong arms, I sighed as his kiss told me more than his words ever could. He loved me. He wasn't going to go back to his ex.

Backing me up into the kitchen, he picked me up and put me on the counter before pulling my sweater off over my head. "What do you say to a little me and you time, baby?"

"Yes," I moaned against his lips. I pulled his sweater off, too, running my hands all over his massive pecs and perfect abs.

Picking me up again, he carried me to the living room this time, putting me on the sofa for a moment while he placed a blanket on the floor in front of us. "I think a little lovemaking in front of the fireplace is in order." I stood, dropping my jeans and stepping out of my shoes. His eyes roamed over me. "Damn, you're as sexy as they come, baby."

Running my hands down my sides, I nodded toward his pants. "Care to drop those?"

He unbuttoned his pants slowly, then let them fall to the floor along with everything else. Naked, the firelight shadowing his body, he looked like a god as he stood there. With one finger, he beckoned me to come to him.

Taking one step at a time, I lost my bra and panties along the way. By the time I reached him, there wasn't a stitch on me. His touch ignited a fire in me that was almost overwhelming. "I'm afraid," I admitted.

"I know." He pulled me close. "I'm sorry about that."

If I knew what would happen, things might not have felt so scary to me. But I didn't know if Tara would win Harman back. I didn't know if her being the mother she needed to be for her son would sway Harman's heart.

Tara would use every tool she had at her disposal—even if that meant using Eli. I knew she would.

But for now, Harman was mine, and I would take advantage of our time together. If it ended, then I would have to deal with the aftermath of that. But for the time being, I had him.

He stroked my cheek softly as we looked into each other's eyes. We didn't have to talk. We both knew things were precarious, that there was nothing more we could say to make things better. Sliding his fingers down my arms, he eased me down to the blanket before moving his body to cover mine.

Moving together, we became one. Nothing had ever felt so good. We moved like waves in a calm sea, exchanging our love in a way I'd never understood before. "Harman, I love you more than I knew possible."

His eyes glistened as he looked down at me. "Don't ever doubt my love for you, Rebel." He kissed me, pushing all the doubt out of my mind for the time being. It wouldn't ever really go away until things were settled.

That fear would always be there in the back of my mind some-where, lurking. And I hated that. I hated the fact that there was someone else who could take my love away.

"I wish I could have faith that this would all end well for us," I confessed, wrapping my arms around him and holding him tight.

Going still, he looked at me with concern. "I guess I should've opened with this, but Tara and I talked today. She confided in me that she doesn't feel right with Eli at her place. It's not like home. So she said she'd try spending more time with him at my place. I'm hoping that will help her get back to her old self with Eli, and then she'll feel comfortable taking him to her place.

"I'm out of this thing. I don't care what you've told her about giving her a chance with me. I'm not giving her that chance. She can be Eli's mother, but she won't be my wife."

"Really?" I wanted to believe him.

Nodding, he leaned in to kiss my lips, and I let it all slip away. All that mattered was that I had him right now. And I made a promise to my body that I'd shut the hell up and let him make me feel the way only he could.

Moving in perfect rhythm again, our kiss went deeper. Sliding back and forth, we couldn't hold back any longer and found our climaxes at the same time.

Panting as we stared into each other's eyes, I knew that he alone would always be my one true love. No one could ever make me feel the way he did. I took his face in my hands, imprinting his handsome face in my brain. "No matter what happens, know I'll never love anyone the way I love you."

"You better not." He smiled, and my heart sped up even more. He kissed the tip of my nose. "And I want you to stop feeling like the rug will be pulled out from under you at any moment. It won't. I promise."

He could make all the promises he wanted to, but I knew it could be yanked out from underneath me. For now, I would pretend to believe him. "I'll try my best to stop acting the way I have been lately." I knew I had to be annoying him by now.

Lifting his heavy body off me, he laid on one side, stroking my stomach as he rested his head on the other hand. "So, Christmas isn't too far away, and I think I would like nothing more than to invite your family over to my place for that."

"Oh, no." I knew it was way too soon for that. And with so much at risk, too—well, there was just no way. "They already have plans."

His wry grin made his eyes sparkle. "Plans that can't be changed? There's still a couple of weeks. And we could do it on Christmas Eve if that would help. I want to meet them. Mom and Dad do, too. They think you and I make a pretty great couple." He leaned over, nibbling my ear, making me giggle.

I pushed his chest. "That tickles."

"It's supposed to." He made a little growling sound, then grazed his teeth down my neck. "Do you think if I bit you, you'd become mine forever? You know, like in that book I saw on your coffee table the other day? The one about the werewolf's mate or something like that."

How I wished that could be true. "You mean, like if I bit you, then no one else could claim what's mine?"

He nodded, suddenly looking serious. "We don't need bloodshed for that to happen. I am yours, Rebel. And you are mine."

I wished I could believe him. But I kept my mouth shut. I didn't see any reason to bring up my doubts. "I am yours." Pulling him to me, I kissed him again.

There'd never been anyone who could kiss my breath away like Harman Hunter could. And I knew there would never be anyone else.

I don't know what I'll do if he ever leaves me.

The sound of his cell ringing had our lips parting as he looked over to his pants. The phone in his pocket made the whole garment shake with the vibrations. "That's Eli's ringtone." Getting up, he went to answer the call.

I heard the sound of a car driving past my house again, too slowly. And when I sat up and looked out the window, I saw Tara's car going by at a snail's pace.

Harman answered his phone, "Hey, Little Buddy, what's up?"

I knew what was up. Eli's mother had left. And she'd done that because Harman wasn't there with her.

I could hear Eli's rushed voice from where I still sat in front of the fireplace. "Mom left. She said it didn't feel the same without you here and that she couldn't do this unless you made her feel at home. Can you come back home? I'll call her and tell her you're coming. Maybe she'll come back then."

I looked at Harman and said the last thing I ever wanted to say to a man I loved as much as I loved him. "Go home, Harman. Make your family whole again."

23

HARMAN

"Stop that, Rebel." I said as soon as I'd ended the call with Eli. I'd had all I could take of her telling me what to do. I was a full-grown man, and I could make my own decisions about the woman I wanted in my life. "I don't want Tara. How much clearer can I be?"

Pulling the blanket around her body to cover herself, Rebel stood, looking at me with such sorrow in her pretty blue eyes. "I know you don't. But your son needs his mother around, and she's obviously not going to be around if you're not. Maybe you can work things out as you go along. But for now, you need to be there when she is if you want your son to have his mother back in his life. And before you say a word, let me tell you that you do want that boy to have his mother back."

I did want that—I'd never denied that. But I didn't know what else I could do about getting Tara back in Eli's life if she didn't want to be. Picking up my pants, I put them on. "I'm going to go home so I can call Tara and find out what her problem is this time." I would've made the call in front of Rebel, but with the way she was acting, I was afraid she'd be onboard with whatever Tara had to say.

"I know exactly what her problem was, Harman." Rebel turned her back to me as she went to pick up her clothes.

Moving in behind her, I took her by the shoulders, turning her to face me. "And what do you think it is?"

"She knew you were here." Blinking fast, she seemed like she was trying not to cry. "Most likely envisioning exactly what we were doing. And it made her feel sick, I bet. She probably felt like she couldn't sit there and pretend that it wasn't happening. And I can't say I blame her. I would feel the same way."

"She doesn't love me." I couldn't keep repeating myself. "And quite frankly, I don't care if her feelings were hurt—that's not an excuse to abandon her son. Whatever she thinks she feels for me— whatever connection she thinks we have because of Eli—is nothing compared to what you and I share."

She moved away from me, heading to the kitchen, and picked up a glass of what looked like soda, downing it in one gulp. "You've got a little boy together, Harman. He may not have been conceived out of love, but you two had him. He's yours *together*. No one should get in the way of that. I love that boy. I truly do." She went to grab something, and I saw when she turned back toward me that she had a bottle of Coke and a bottle of Jack Daniel's in her hands.

"Did you just gulp an entire glass of Jack and Coke just now?" I shook my head in disbelief. Rebel wasn't a big drinker, and by the looks of it, I was turning her into one.

"Maybe." She filled half the glass with straight Jack then splashed some Coke into it before adding some ice cubes.

I went straight over to her, took the glass out of her hand and poured it in the sink. "No, ma'am. I will not allow this. You can't do this to yourself. I'll deal with things. You'll see. It'll all work out. Maybe not exactly like you want it to, but it will work out. And you don't need to turn into an alcoholic because of me. That would destroy me."

"And this is destroying me, Harman." Slowly, she sank down to the floor until she sat on it, looking pitiful. "I'm robbing a little boy of his mother." Her tear-filled eyes came up to meet mine. "*We're* robbing a little boy of his mother, Harman."

I hadn't felt that way. But hearing her say it made my heart stop. *Have I put myself before my son?*

I'd never done that before. Not since the moment I knew I was going to be a father, had I ever put myself first. And here I was, letting him down for the first time ever. And I could only blame love for that inexcusable action.

Putting on the rest of my clothes, I looked at Rebel as she sat on the floor, staring at the tiles with glazed eyes. "I'm sorry."

"Just go." She fell over and wrapped the blanket around her tightly. "This isn't anyone's fault. There's no reason to say that you're sorry."

But there was a reason. I knew my situation with Tara was a precarious one. I'd always told myself that I would take her back, so we could be a family again. I'd lied to myself about that.

My son came first. And he needed both his mother and father—but not like this. "Look, Tara's the one who needs to understand things," I grasped at straws. "I'm not going to let her use my own son to blackmail me into a relationship that neither of us has any business being in."

"Whatever. Do what you think you have to," Rebel mumbled then hiccupped.

The one drink had done her in. Scooping her up, I carried her to her bed and laid her down. "Sleep it off, baby. I'll come back to check on you after I put Eli to bed. And I'll figure something out."

Closing her eyes, she whispered, "I love you, and I love Eli, and I just want to do what's right for you both. 'Night."

I picked her keys up off the dresser since I'd be back later and locked up Rebel's house behind me. Then I headed home to try to figure out what I needed to do about this mess we'd all gotten into.

Finding Eli in his bedroom staring at the television, I asked, "So, it went pretty crappy then?"

"The crappiest, Dad." Eli sat up then picked up the television remote, turning it off to give me his undivided attention. "Mom came in and was acting like she'd never been in this house before. It was like she didn't know what to do or something. She didn't sit down at all the whole time. Just kept looking out the window. She told me you were coming in right behind her and that you guys had talked, and she'd be coming over a lot more. She said she might even be moving in—and that made me super happy."

And there it was. My son had just told me exactly what would make him happy. *What's a devoted father supposed to do with that information? Ignore it?*

The only thing I didn't understand was why Tara had thought I was coming in right behind her. I'd never said I was. What I'd told her was that she could see Eli at my house. I'd made it perfectly clear that I wasn't part of the deal. "I need to call your mom. We've got to get some things straight."

"Dad?" he asked as I turned to leave.

Stopping, I looked back at him. "Yeah?"

"I want Mom back. I want her here with me." His eyes drooped. "Can't you guys just get along?"

My heart stopped, and my stomach knotted, and I'd never felt so selfish in my life. "We can do that, Little Buddy."

Leaving him with a smile on his face, I went to my study to make the call to Tara. There had to be something we could do to make our son happy.

She answered on the third ring, "You still with her?"

"No." I leaned back in the office chair as I sat behind the desk. "Why'd you leave?"

"I can't do this without you. I never could." She made a loud sigh. "Harman, I need you. I've always needed you where our son was concerned. You know that. Now, what are you going to do about it?"

"There's a ton of room in this place. Maybe you could live here, and we could figure out how to live in the same place and get along for Eli's sake but still live separate lives." Closing my eyes, I knew that if Tara moved into my home, it might not be something Rebel could handle. But I had to work things out for my son first.

"You don't understand, Harman. I *need* you. I don't want to live there and live separate lives. I want us to be a family again. You know what I'm saying, don't you?" she asked.

I'd heard enough. "Listen Tara, if you don't know how to be a parent on your own, then that's on you. I have been begging you to see a therapist for years. Now you're saying you won't be a mother to our son unless I—what? Marry you again? Do you think that's any better for our son? Us getting together and breaking up again—and we will break up again—than us being apart and being good co-parents? How is an unhappy marriage any better of an environment for him?

"If you want to be in our lives, then this is what's going to happen. You will move in to one of the suites in this house, and you will learn how to be a mother to your child. But I am not a part of that deal. I will help you as much as I can as Eli's father, but I will not marry you again." I had reached the end of my rope, and I didn't know how else to make things right.

The stunned silence on the other end of the line was as satisfying as it was surprising. But it didn't last long. "If I move in with you, I don't want *her* around," Tara finally replied.

"You want me to give up Rebel." I knew what she wanted, but I wasn't going to give her everything so easily. I meant it when I said I wouldn't be getting back together with Tara, but I could only hope that Rebel could be patient. She didn't need to be involved in this mess, and I needed time to fix my family. I could only hope that Rebel would still be there once I got it all sorted.

"Of course, I do. How would it look with us living together and you and her still seeing each other?" she asked with a whiny tone to her voice. "Harman, I don't want to become a laughing stock. I would think you wouldn't want Rebel to become one either."

Would that actually happen?

I didn't care what anyone else thought, except for Rebel. And even as I tried to tell myself differently, I knew Rebel wouldn't continue seeing me if Tara took me up on what I was proposing. "That shouldn't matter. The only thing that matters is Eli."

"I agree," she said. "And having his biological parents together is what's best for him. It's what's best for any child. My parents have said that all along. They'll be so happy we're getting back together. It's time we both stop being selfish and do what's right for the only one who matters here. That's Eli. It's not you, me, or Rebel. It's only him."

"Tara, we are not getting back together. How would that work anyway, once he's old enough to move out? You know you and I wouldn't have any excuse to stay together," I told her. "What then?" The longer this conversation went on, the more I remembered just how manipulative Tara could be. I wouldn't let her get the best of me. "No. It's best if you just move in and put any notion of us and a future out of your mind."

"We could deal with those problems when the time comes." She went quiet for a minute. "We need to do what will make our son happy, Harman. I'll move in, but you have to give Rebel up. No dating. Give me a chance to show you that it's best for us all to be a family together."

My jaw ached from holding it so tight. My head hurt from thinking so damn much. And my mouth opened but nothing came out of it. I didn't want Tara back. I didn't want to even see her every day in my home. I looked out the window, seeing Rebel's house glowing in the distance. Would I give her up?

Will I be able to?

Her voice but a whisper, she said, "Harman, I can't change what I've done. I can only try harder to make the future better."

I had to admit that Tara had matured a hell of a lot in the last month. But would that be enough on its own? "And what changes *are* you going to make?"

She cleared her throat, and I realized that she'd been crying silently. "I'll sell the shop and devote myself to our son and you."

Throughout the years, I'd known how much the pregnancy had affected her mentally, how it had made her feel like she had no choices. "I don't want you to give up working if you like it." I swallowed hard, knowing what I had to say next, but hating myself for it. "And I'll break things off with Rebel on one condition, Tara. You've got to start seeing a therapist. One of my choosing."

She'd always rejected the idea, and I knew if she rejected it again, there was no hope for our family—whatever our family was. "If you'll join me in couple's therapy, I'll see your therapist, Harman. I'm serious this time. I want to make things work. I want to do that for our son. He never asked for this. You and I made that mistake on our own."

"It wasn't a mistake." I hated when that even went through my mind. "Eli wasn't a mistake. No matter what else happened before or since, he wasn't a mistake."

"Then neither were we," she said with a long sigh punctuating her remark. "I'm just now realizing that for the first time ever, Harman. *We* weren't a mistake. Something brought us together that night. We might've only had that one night, but it gave us Eli."

You couldn't even call it a night. It was ten minutes. But she was right. It had given us Eli. Both of us. Not just her. Not just me. Both of us. And he deserved to have us both.

Even if that meant I had to give up Rebel.

I sighed into the phone, and I imagined I could almost hear my heart breaking. "Okay. I will see a family counselor with you—but we will remain separated. And I'll stop seeing Rebel for as long as we remain in counseling. That is the best I can do right now, Tara."

I could practically hear Tara's smile through the phone; the woman always got what she wanted, and I imagine that's what she thought was happening here. She may have matured, but a person can only change so much.

"Deal," she said. "I can move in tomorrow."

24

REBEL

WAKING UP WITH A POUNDING HEADACHE, I opened my eyes to see Harman walking into my room. "Where've you been?" I didn't recall a whole lot after he got the call from Eli.

He stood there across the room, looking so sad and not coming any closer. "Home." He put the keys on my dresser. "I took your keys. I didn't want to leave the door unlocked, and knew I had to come back to check on you. By the way, I've poured out the rest of the bottle of Jack Daniel's. It was a precautionary measure."

"I need something for this headache." I climbed out of bed, then realized I had no clothes on. "Oh, hell."

Harman grabbed my robe off the hook, tossing it to me. "Here you go. Put that on."

My lack of clothing had never bothered him before. I instantly felt sick to my stomach—and I didn't think it had anything to do with the hangover. "Do you mind filling me in on what happened with that phone call you got? I've kind of forgotten about it."

"Yeah, a whole glass of Jack and very little Coke will do that to a person." He gave me a serious look. "Hey, promise me you won't use that stuff to get over me."

My hands, which had been struggling with the belt on my robe, fell to my sides. "What?"

"Promise me that you won't take to drinking, Rebel," he said, leaving out the most important part.

"What's going on, Harman?" I sat on the bed. My head felt so light that I thought I might faint. I had to sit down or risk falling. "You said something about me getting over you. What's that about?"

"She's going to move in with me and get therapy." He shifted his weight, looking nervous. "This is over." I'd told myself a million times that this is how it would end, but it hadn't helped me one bit.

It felt like someone had reached into my chest and ripped my heart right out. Nothing had ever hurt this bad, and I prayed nothing ever would again.

Harman just kept repeating the same words over and over again: "I'm sorry." That's all I heard for at least ten minutes as I cried like a baby.

"I know you have to do this." I stopped to wail. "I know it's best for Eli." I fell back on the bed, thinking I might be having a heart attack it hurt so badly.

"Baby!" Harman was suddenly right there, holding me. I wished he hadn't touched me.

But I clung to him, holding him so tightly, as if I could hold my shattered world together if I just held him tight enough. "Don't end this! Please!"

His lips pressed against my forehead. "I've got to. I've been selfish, and I've got to stop."

And that one word hit me right where it should've. I was being selfish, too. "I'm sorry." Now it was my turn to say those words over and over. "I never wanted to come between you guys." But I had done just that.

Harman left me alone and I tried to take a few minutes to compose myself. He came back with some pain reliever and a glass of water. "Here, take these."

Wiping the tears out of my eyes, I tried to make light of the situation. "Doctor's orders?"

Nodding, he said, "Doctor's orders. And I want to make a few more while I'm at it. No more crying. I still love you. You'll never lose that. There is no one else I'd rather be with—and I hope I never lose your love either. But things have to be this way. For now. Maybe forever. Because I've been selfish with you, too. So incredibly selfish, and I hope you can forgive me. But it's not because I don't love you. You just don't deserve to be a part of this mess. And until I can get my family sorted out, I don't deserve you either."

"I love you, too. I always will, I think." I thought about Eli as I swallowed the pills, hoping they'd be able to take away my headache and my heartache for good. "And I love Eli. He's going to have his family back. I'm happy for him."

"Yeah, me too." Happiness was the last word I would have used to describe how Harman sounded. He looked at my open bedroom door. "I should go. Are you going to be okay?"

Not even close.

Nodding, I didn't want to put any more guilt on him. He had more than his fair share already. "I've got a doctor's order for you, too, Harman."

"And that is?" he asked as he moved slowly toward the door.

"You make the best family you can for that boy." I gulped back the knot that formed in my throat. "He deserves a great family. He's a great kid. And please, let him know that I won't need his help with the animals. It'll make his mother upset if he keeps coming around, but I don't think I'd be able to tell him that myself without breaking down."

"Yeah, I know." Harman backed out the door. "I'll explain things to him. He wants his family back—he told me that. He'll have to understand that it means he can't come here anymore. He'll have to understand that having his mother back means losing you."

"No one gets to have it all," I whispered as I watched his eyes glaze over.

A tear ran down his cheek. "Yeah, no one gets to have it all. I suppose love wasn't in the cards for me. Not a love I'd get to keep, anyway."

"You'll always have my love, Harman. My heart is yours." I saw no reason to lie to the man. He held my heart in the palm of his hand; maybe it would be a comfort to him as he laid in his cold bed with Tara.

Don't think about it, I told myself, even as my heart shattered into even tinier pieces.

More tears fell from his eyes. "You've got mine, too. I've got to go. Sorry." He turned and left in a rush. I heard the door close.

Burying my face in the pillow, I let myself cry. Doctor's orders or not, I was going to have to cry. I knew I had to let it all out somehow.

What I didn't know was how long that would take. Sleep didn't come that night, and I had to call in sick the next day. Another night passed without a wink of sleep, and I cried a hell of a lot, too.

One more day of calling in sick, and I finally stopped crying. But I couldn't make myself get out of my robe—the one Harman had tossed me when he'd come to break my heart. I hadn't bathed, brushed my teeth, or my hair. I felt like the walking dead.

That third day, I sat on my sofa, looking out the window. When I saw Tara's car pass by, I felt it all come up again, and I fell apart once more. I promised myself that would be the last time.

She had her family back. I'd lost what had become mine, but at least they were whole again. And I had to stop being so selfish. I had to pick myself up and dust myself off and get on with my life.

When a knock came to my door, I just looked at it from my safe spot on the sofa. "Who is it?" I finally asked.

"Tara."

Why is she here?

To rub it in? I got up and went to the door, not caring that I looked like a truck had run me over. She needed to know what she'd done to me.

And just as I was about to let her see what I'd become, I stopped myself. "I'm sick, Tara. Now's not a good time. I think I've got the flu. I don't want you to catch it."

It wasn't her fault that I'd fallen in love with a man who'd told me straight up that he'd give his ex-wife another chance if she wanted to make their family whole. So I wasn't going to try to make her feel guilty about what had happened to me.

"Oh, that's too bad," she called out through the door, sounding much too cheerful. "I'll have Rene bring you some chicken soup. She can leave it on your doorstep. I'll stop by in a few days to see how you're doing. I just wanted to let you know that I'm seeing a therapist. Harman found one for me. And we're seeing a marriage counselor, too. I know you probably don't want to hear about that, but I wanted to let you know that I'm trying, Rebel. I really am."

"That's good to hear." I leaned on the door, feeling terrible about everything. "I miss them both," I mumbled, almost more to myself than anyone else. "Don't tell them that," I rushed to add, "but I do. And I'm glad you're getting help. It does help to talk to someone who can help you with what you've gone through." And then I knew I needed help, too. "I'm gonna go see someone, too."

"Good," she said with a happy lilt to her voice. "I know this has to be hard on you."

It's killing me.

But Eli was who mattered the most. "Yeah, it is. But as long as Eli's happy, that's all I care about."

"Yeah, us too." She made two knocks on the door. "I'll let you get back to it then, Rebel. Listen for Rene's knock to get your soup. And I'm sorry it has to be this way."

I was sort of sick of how many *sorrys* I'd said and heard lately.

Stumbling back to the sofa, I looked at it but didn't sit down. I needed a bath, and I needed to get off my pity pony. Sure, I'd lost the love of my life, but a little boy had his mommy and daddy back under the same roof.

As I stripped off the robe—which I tossed into the trashcan as I walked past the kitchen—I found myself wondering if Tara was sleeping in the same bed Harman and I had.

My stomach began to hurt even more, and I had to stop thinking about that. It didn't matter where she slept. Harman wasn't mine anymore. He was trying to be a good husband and father, and I needed to let him do that. Not that I could stop him if I'd wanted to.

I wanted them to be happy. If they could be happy. *Can they really be happy?*

Turning on the water, I got into the shower, washing the remnants of our last time together off my body. Some would've thought it disgusting to live that way for three damn days. And they'd be right. But until that moment, I couldn't just wash away what was left of the man I loved.

Running my soapy hands over my belly, I wondered what would've happened if I'd gotten pregnant. Would Harman have felt the same way about everything?

It didn't matter. I wasn't pregnant. I'd been on the shot for years. No little miracle would come along to keep us connected for the rest of our lives, the way Eli had connected Harman and Tara. And I wouldn't have wanted that to be the only thing keeping us together anyway.

The truth was, I felt sorry for Tara. She would never know real, genuine love—not the kind Harman and I shared. I felt it there still, beating in my broken heart. We'd always love one another, even if we could never be together.

There were worse things than sacrificing love, so a child could have the life he deserved. Did it nearly kill me? Yes. But no sacrifice ever comes easy.

25

HARMAN

THE FOURTH DAY seemed to be the hardest day yet. I'd woken up with a hard-on after dreaming all night long about Rebel. To say I missed her didn't come close to describing how I felt.

I could stop picturing Rebel as she collapsed into tears. I'd tried to explain everything when the first onslaught had come, but I didn't think she'd heard a thing I said. I'd told her that it didn't have to mean the end, that I wasn't actually getting back together with Tara, just cohabitating with her. But as I'd watched her body being overtaken by wracking sobs, I knew I hadn't been fair to Rebel.

I couldn't keep stringing her along with promises that things would be better some day. It was selfish of me to hope that she'd wait around until I was able to help Tara become the mother she needed to be. Rebel deserved to be happy, too, and I knew she'd never move on if she didn't get the closure she needed.

So I hadn't repeated the bit about staying separated from Tara and had just let Rebel assume the worst. And the days since had been some of the worst of my life.

Tara had moved into the servant's suite, putting her place up for sale. She was giving it her all just as she'd said she would. And she was about to have her first session with the therapist I'd set her up with. And we were set up with another counselor to start our family therapy on the first of the year. Things were in place to help us become a stronger family unit for Eli. But nothing we'd done so far had me feeling like we were any closer to becoming the family we all wanted to be.

Something was missing. And I knew that something was the love Rebel had brought to Eli and I. Tara just didn't have the natural knack for making people feel loved that Rebel had. Not that Tara tried too hard to make anyone feel great.

In fact, I'd almost go so far as to say that Tara had the exact opposite effect on people. She'd come into our home and turned our world upside down. Eli had a new bedtime—eight o'clock sharp. And Tara stayed firm with the no drinking after five each evening. She acted as if Eli hadn't gotten over his bedwetting stage, no matter how many times he and I had told her. Even the maid who took care of his linens told Tara he hadn't had an accident in two years.

I thought it was kind of funny that Eli's bedwetting had stopped almost immediately after Tara had moved out. I never pointed that out to her, though. And any time I tried to fight her on her new rules, she'd just start up with the dramatics, and I didn't have the energy to put up with that. Not when I was spending so much energy trying to heal my broken heart.

And with Tara back, all the reasons I'd never been able to give my heart to my wife came flying back to my mind.

Tara didn't try to get anyone to love her. She was who she was, take her or leave her—there was no room for compromise. And I preferred the latter. But Eli was happy that she was back.

Catching him in the hallway as we were both going down to breakfast, I saw a smile on his lips. "You're looking pretty happy today, Little Buddy."

Nodding, he skipped ahead of me. "It just makes me happy to know that Mom's in the breakfast room, and I get to see her each morning before I go to school."

And that was the reason I was doing any of this. I knew if this was to work, I had to start communicating with Tara about how I wanted things done in my home. Not that I'd call it mine, because I wanted her to think of it as hers, too. But the fact was, she'd come in and taken over, and neither Eli nor I were happy about the changes she'd made.

Patting Eli on the back, I let him in on my plan, "I'm glad you like having your mom here. But I think it's time I dealt with these crazy new rules she's come up with."

"Good." He hopped down the stairs. "The no-drinking-after-five and the no-swimming-before-bed need to go, Dad. And I think the homework-done-as-soon-as-I-get-home should go, too."

"Now that one, I agree with." It was a lot better having Eli get his homework done right away than it had been for me to get home and have to help him with it.

"Aw, man," he whined.

Walking into the breakfast room, we saw Tara sitting at the table with her iPad. She tore her gaze away, looking up at us. "Good morning, boys."

Eli ran over to kiss her cheek, and I went to pour myself a cup of coffee. Though I knew she was trying her best to try to rekindle things between us—despite me being firmly against it—there had been no reconnecting. Not that I had expected there to be; we'd never had passion in our marriage, even at the best of times. I didn't expect it to magically appear, like she seemed to. It was enough for me to simply try to be civil and caring, especially in front of Eli. "Morning, Tara. I hope you slept well."

"I did." She ran her hand through Eli's hair. "I think today we'll stop and get you a haircut after school."

"Or I could let Rebel cut it," he said. "She's great at it."

Tara's eyes narrowed, and she looked at me for help, but I just dodged her gaze, looking at the tray of food on the side table. "Rene has outdone herself with this morning's treats. Look, Eli, pigs in a blanket."

"Yes!" He shot over to my side, picking up a plate and putting a couple of his favorite foods on it. "And look, there's some with ham in them, too."

"There sure is." I took my plate then went to sit at the table.

"I'm going to stop by my place and pick up some more things today," Tara told me. "And I've ordered a kennel for the dog. He needs to stay outside from now on."

Eli's face dropped. "Mom, he sleeps in my room. He's not running around the house. Please don't make me keep him outside."

"Dogs don't belong in the house, Eli. You've got to learn that." She gave me the stink-eye. "Your father knew better than to let you keep an animal in the house."

"He keeps Moppy clean, Tara. The dog's never been a problem. He's house-trained, and he never gets into any trouble. I think the dog's fine the way he is now." I looked at Eli and overrode his mother's new rule. "He can stay inside, Eli." Then I turned my attention to Tara. "And there's no need for a kennel. I don't want Moppy locked up when he's outside. He's got so much space to roam around that it would be cruel."

The way she looked down at her half-eaten plate told me she wasn't happy that I'd pushed back. "Fine."

Eli's cell went off, and he got up, taking one of the pastries with him. "Jason and his mom are here. I've gotta go." He kissed his mother on the cheek, then gave me a hug and off he went.

That left Tara and me alone. "So, how's the suite working out for you, Tara?"

"It's okay. A little on the small side, but okay." She sipped her coffee, looking at me over the rim. "Maybe after seeing the therapist for a while, we'll feel like getting back to sleeping in the same bed again."

I knew that wouldn't be the case. She'd made plenty of comments in the few short days she'd been there, and I always shut them down. This time I simply gave her a look, making it clear once again that I wasn't interested in that.

The thought of sleeping with any other woman while I still carried so much love in my heart for Rebel made me sick. I kept hoping it would slowly go away, but I didn't honestly believe it would.

"Harman, how long can we live this way?"

"You seem to forget that we lived this way for a long time. Most of our marriage was like this, the two of us living separate lives. I don't see why we can't do it again," I didn't know what else to tell her. "But while we're on the subject of making do together, I'd like to bring up some of the things you've decided to change around here. The no-drinking-after-five rule has to stop. The kid's thirsty, Tara. When he gets up, he gulps down two bottles of water. I can't let that go on. And the no-swimming-before-bed needs to go, too."

She looked as if she'd be putting her foot down about that. "No, Harman. It's too stimulating for him. It'll make it hard for him to fall asleep."

"It *helps* him get to sleep. If you had let him swim with me that first night you stayed here, you'd have seen that," I pointed out.

Her jaw set, she got that determined look in her green eyes. "I'll let the after five thing go, but not the swimming."

Leaning back in my chair, I had to ask, "Why are you doing this, Tara?"

"Doing what?" she asked, all innocence, as if she had no idea what the hell I was talking about.

"Coming in here and trying to change everything," I told her. "Eli and I were doing just fine—"

"Without me," she interrupted me. "Yes, I know." Getting up, she went to stand by the window, holding the cup of coffee in her hands. "Her car hasn't left the driveway in four days."

I knew Rebel's car hadn't left her driveway. And I was pretty sure I knew why, too. She didn't have a kid she had to stay strong for. Rebel had the time and privacy to indulge in the pain of our breakup. I hurt, too, more than I ever could have imagined. But I had to keep that hidden, buried deep down inside.

"I'm sure she'll be okay, given enough time." I didn't want to talk to my ex about the woman I still loved.

Turning to face me, Tara looked a little sheepish. "I stopped by there yesterday."

"Why?" I demanded, my entire being tensing up at the thought.

"After all she's been through—everything you've put her through—I think it's best to leave her alone."

"She missed you and Eli; she told me not to tell you. But I think you should know." She sipped her coffee as if we were having the most casual conversation. "She said she has the flu, but I think it's a broken heart that has her missing work." Looking down at the table, I caught her looking at me. "And how's your heart, Harman?"

"There's no reason to discuss this, Tara." I had no idea what her angle was, but I didn't want to discuss my shattered heart with her.

"I want to know how you feel, Harman." Moving away from the window, she took a seat.

"Tara, I truly love Rebel. I told you that. I doubt I'll ever stop loving her." I didn't know why Tara would want to hear about my feelings for another woman, but I refused to hide them from her.

A smile curved her lips. "Wow."

I didn't trust that smile. "Yeah, I know," I replied, narrowing my eyes at her.

"And you truly love our son, too." She sipped the coffee again. "You left her for him, so he could have his family back. That's the most selfless thing I've ever heard."

It was nothing compared to Rebel's selflessness. And I didn't want her bothered by any of us anymore. "Tara, please don't go by Rebel's place anymore. She's been through too much from our family already."

"I agree." Putting her cup down, she ran her hands over her blouse to straighten it. "We're a mess. And we've splattered our mess on her."

"Exactly. We are a mess. I should've known better than to start anything with the woman in the first place. It wasn't fair to her."

"Yeah." She got up and left the room, leaving me sitting there alone.

I moved to look out the window. There wasn't any smoke coming from Rebel's chimney. She'd just holed herself up in that house, and there wasn't a thing I could do about it.

Seeing her again would only prolong the pain. The wound cut

deep but left alone it would heal. If I or anyone in my family kept going around Rebel, it'd take her longer to recover. Keeping Eli from her might not be so easy, though.

Rene came into the breakfast room. "Are you finished, Doctor Hunter?"

"I am." I handed her my barely eaten plate. "Here you go."

She looked at all the food left over. "You guys aren't eating as much as you normally do. I guess this is as hard on you all as it is on Rebel."

That piqued my curiosity. "You say that like you've seen her recently."

"Tara asked me take Rebel some soup yesterday," she said as she gathered the dishes. "She invited me in and we chatted a bit. She said she'd finally gotten herself cleaned up a bit, but she hadn't done anything but feed and water her animals for three days. I could see the weight loss in her face. I told her things would get better with time."

Rene had been with us since we'd moved into the house. She knew my family better than anyone else did. "Is this a mistake, Rene?"

She looked at me without any expression on her face at all. "We all make mistakes, Doctor Hunter. And we all walk different paths in life. There's no one way to live. If you feel like you need to have Eli's mother here for your son to have the best possible life, then that's what you should do."

"If you were in my shoes, what would you do?" I had to hear someone else's opinion. I hadn't confided in anyone else.

She laughed lightly as she headed out of the room with the dishes. "Me? Oh, I'm a romantic, Doctor Hunter. I lead with my heart, not my head." And then she left.

26

REBEL

SOMEHOW I GOT through an entire week without speaking to Harman or Eli. I didn't feel any better. Not a bit. But I had managed to make it into work and had even worked the weekend, something I'd rarely done since moving in next door to Eli and Harman. They'd taken up most of my weekends since then.

Nancy, my coworker, came into my office with a grin on her face. "Looks like you and I are in charge of planning the office Christmas party this year, Rebel. I'm thinking copious amounts of booze and one of those white elephant gift exchanges."

"Sounds great to me. That's easy to plan." I couldn't muster the enthusiasm to be excited about a party.

Nancy seemed to sense that. "Well, there's a lot more to plan. The food, the place, the time, the date. How about I come over to your place when we get off today? I'll bring wine and a cheeseboard. I'd invite you over, but my place is a zoo. Not with animals, but with people. Besides, I'm dying to see your new place."

I knew Nancy well enough to know she wouldn't give up until I caved. "Okay. I'll text you the address. I can pick up something, too, if you want."

"Nah, I got this. Consider it a housewarming gift." She left me, happy to have gotten her way.

Later, as I drove home after work, I pulled into my driveway just as Tara passed behind me. She tooted her horn and waved, smiling happily. I raised my hand, not much of a wave, but not ignoring her either.

It seemed things were going great at the Hunter household. At least, it looked that way judging by the smile I'd seen on her face. Heading inside, I went to the back to take care of the animals before Nancy arrived.

My doorbell rang just as I finished up in the back, and I hurried to answer it. Nancy's smile and a bottle of wine greeted me. "I've got the goods."

Letting her in, I stepped back. I even managed a smile. "Come in. I've just finished my chores, and I'm free to plan with you." Heading to the kitchen, I added, "I'll grab a couple of wine glasses."

With nothing left to do, I took a seat while Nancy fished out the wine opener and set out the cheeseboard. "I've got to say, you've got the gift, Nancy. They picked the right party planner in you. Me, I'm not so sure about. But they've got a gem in you."

"Right? I really do love planning—especially parties. I think you'll love this wine, by the way." She filled our glasses and took the seat opposite me, pulling out a pen and a pad of paper from her purse. "I'm prepared to take down the notes of this meeting." She laughed. "Sorry, I just never get to have meetings anymore since I left the law firm to take over the bookkeeping at the clinic."

I didn't know much about Nancy and took the opportunity to get to know her better. "Why did you leave a cushy job like that, if you don't mind my asking?"

"Well, I worked way too many hours there." She leaned back, taking another drink of the wine. "When I married Harry I had to transition to something that wasn't so time-consuming. So, I went from being a lawyer's assistant to being the bookkeeper at the clinic."

"Why'd you have to work less?" I asked, then picked up some cheese to nibble on.

"He had two kids," she said, as if that meant anything to me. "You know, he needed my help with them."

"And their mother?" I asked, thinking that should've been her job, not Nancy's.

"She works, too." She picked up a grape and popped it into her mouth. "I love these cheeseboard thingys."

"Well, how did you come into play in that whole thing?" I asked. "I mean, you're just their stepmother."

"Honey, I'm not *just* a stepparent. I'm a *parent* to those kids. I love them like they're my own." She pointed at the small row of meats. "Try one of those; they're smoked to perfection."

I picked up some of what she'd pointed out, feeling like I had an appetite for the first time in a week. And I desperately wanted to hear more about her family situation. "Do you get along with Harry's ex?"

"We did not get along well at all, at first." She took another drink of wine. "They'd only been divorced for a year, and I think she was kind of surprised he'd found someone to put up with the things she couldn't stand. Harry's a bit of a sloppy person. She hated that about him. I don't care so much. And I'm picking up after everyone else anyway, so I don't think it's a big deal."

"She left him because he's sloppy?" I thought that sounded rather shallow.

"No, she left him because they no longer loved each other." Taking another sip of the wine, she asked, "If I get too tipsy will it be okay to leave my car here overnight? I'll take a cab home. This is going down a little too easy, but I don't want to stop."

"Of course, you can leave your car here. It's not a problem at all." Knowing that Nancy had stepkids and had learned to deal with an ex-wife, I knew I had to get more information out of her. "So, your husband's ex never wanted to get back together with him for their kids' sakes?"

"No." She looked rather confused. "Why would she? She left him, and he was fine with that. They'd grown apart."

From the way Harman told it, he and his ex had never been that close, but he'd taken her back. I felt the urge to unburden myself about my own issues, hoping Nancy would be able to lend a sympathetic ear. I'd been so tight-lipped about my private life for the most part, and I'd forgotten how good it felt to share with someone. "I've been seeing this guy. He's got a little boy—he's eight. So, this man I've been seeing only married his ex-wife because she was pregnant; they were never in love, and they never fell in love during their six-year marriage.

"She left him a couple of years ago, and he'd never dated until me. And we fell in love—quick. But he'd told me before we started dating that if his ex wanted to come back, he'd let her. He felt it was important for their son to do that."

"Well, that's stupid." Nancy rolled her eyes.

"Is it?" No one else had seemed to think so—least of all, Tara. In a way, it seemed like the right thing to do.

"It is." She took another drink, so I did, too. "No good marriage ever ends in divorce—and why should two people who don't make each other happy stay together just for the children? Or child, in their case. It's not for the child, I can tell you that. Children are perceptive. Even if they don't feel it at the time, when they get older, they'll realize that their parents didn't have a good relationship. Then these kids are saddled with the knowledge that they were the reason their parents lives were so miserable. No, whoever said that couples should stay together for the kids was severely misguided—I saw that not only as stepparent, but as a child of miserable parents. Tell your guy not to entertain any thoughts about letting his ex back in. Unless he really does have feelings for her, that is."

After another sip, I asked, "And if his ex asked me to back off so she could win her kid back—she's been pretty neglectful of him lately—then what?"

"Now her kid is a different story. You've got to give that boy's mother room to be his mother. Don't try to take over her role. But you can take on your own motherly role if the kid wants you to." She picked up a piece of cheese, wagging it as she went on. "If you love a man, you accept his kids. It's a package deal. And sometimes that package comes along with an ex you have to learn to care about, too.

Her feelings matter, too, and you don't want to step on any mother's toes."

Finishing the glass of wine, I leaned up to refill it. "I don't want to step on her toes. She was really young when she got pregnant. I don't think she ever really developed that motherly instinct. My guy was about six years older than her, and she let him take the main parental role mostly. That's what it sounded like to me, anyway." I took another sip of wine, wondering if there was anything that could be done to fix my situation, or if it truly was time for me to move on.

Raising her eyebrows, Nancy asked, "So she counts on the boy's father to do most of the raising then?"

"Yes." Tara definitely counted on Harman way more than most mothers did. I was sure of that. Harman easily took on more than half of the share of parental responsibility. "She acted as though as long as the boy had his father, things were pretty good, and she didn't need to be as present. But then I came along, and her son became attached to me. And it bothered her."

"I bet it did," Nancy said as she nodded. "Sometimes it takes another person stepping into your role to realize what a sub-par job you're doing. But this is where your patience comes into play, Rebel. If this woman wants to step up now and make up for her earlier carelessness, then you can't stand in the way of that. If that boy is already attached to you, then she could see that as a threat and become a real problem."

"Yeah, she already has." I found myself drinking until the glass was empty. The wine sure was going down smooth.

"What's she done?" She looked a bit worried, probably because I'd consumed a whole glass of wine in under a minute.

"She told her ex that she wants it all back—him, the kid, their home." I hiccupped then laughed hysterically. "And she did, just like that," I snapped my fingers to punctuate my point. "She got it all back!"

"No." Nancy got up and came to hug me. "Honey, I'm so sorry. This isn't good at all."

"No, it's not. It's awful, and that's why I was out for four days this week. It's killing me. I love him and his son so much, and every part of me is hurting. I haven't got to see them in seven days now. And it's not getting any easier." I felt the tears beginning to burn the backs of my eyes. I didn't want to cry anymore. I wanted to get better. I wanted to get over Harman and Eli, but I couldn't.

Nancy took charge. "Okay, does this man love you? Like, really love you, Rebel?"

"He does. I know he does." If only it were that simple. "And *I* told him to fix his family. I didn't fight for him; I thought it would be best for his son. I love that kid and want to see him happy."

"Was he happy when you and his dad were together?" she asked me as she gauged my reaction.

"He was. I know he was. Even before I got together with his father, Eli was happy hanging around here. He helped me look after the animals—he loved it. It was his mother. She felt too threatened by me, but I never wanted to try to take her place—I even spoke to her a couple times before I got together with Harman, asking her to spend time with Eli." My emotions were all over the place, and it was becoming harder and harder not to place a lot of the blame for the entire situation squarely on Tara's shoulders. "And I don't even know now if she's really got Eli's best interests at heart. I think she thinks that if she's a good mom, she'll be able to win her ex over. And she might be right about that, too. But she came to me and told me she would be there for Eli—that she'd be able to bring her family together if I just got out of the way."

"Well. Quite frankly, the woman sounds insufferable," Nancy let me know. "It sounds like she's got it all mixed up; she should be able to be a good mother whether she's with her ex or not, and whether her son has found another adult to look up to or not. If you and this man love each other, then she needs to respect that. And if her son has fun coming around her and helping you with the animals, then she needs to respect that too. Sounds like that's what would be in the son's best interest, in my opinion. She can't keep her ex hostage in a loveless relationship just because she's jealous of your connection to their son."

"Yeah," I nodded my head, things finally clicking into place in a way that made sense. "I think you're right, Nancy." I sat up with renewed energy, grateful to be able to brush off my forlorn way of thinking. "She needs to respect our love. It shouldn't make a difference to her relationship with her son; she can see her son as much as she wants, but the relationship I have with his father needs to be respected. Or at least tolerated. Yeah."

"You're damn right it does." Nancy filled my glass again. "So, I expect you to talk some sense into your man before things get any worse for you guys. But for now, let's plan this Christmas party."

27

HARMAN

NOT LONG AFTER I'd gotten into bed, my cell rang, and the ringtone told me who it was before I even saw the screen. My body reacted instantly. My heart sped up, and my cock sprang to life. "Rebel? Is everything okay?" concern etched my voice, as I knew she wouldn't have called unless it was something important.

"Not really," she said quietly. "Things could be better. I miss you and Eli more than I knew possible."

"We miss you, too." He'd just asked me if I'd spoken to Rebel when I put him to bed earlier. When I told him that I hadn't, he'd looked away sadly before wishing me goodnight.

"Harman, can you talk right now?" she asked. "You know, is Tara with you?"

"No, she's not. We don't share a bedroom, Rebel." I thought she might have thought Tara and I had gone back to married life, which we hadn't.

"This is selfish of me, but I'm glad about that." She made a heavy sigh before going on, "I talked to a lady I work with. She's got stepkids and has to deal with an ex-wife. It was great getting to talk to someone who's been through a similar situation. She gave me some good advice, Harman."

"And that is?" I asked, curious about what someone who'd been in that position would have to offer.

"Staying together for your kids isn't the right thing to do," Rebel let me know.

Unfortunately our situation was a bit more complicated than that. "I know. But having Tara close right now—it's the only thing I can think to do. This is what Eli wants."

"I know." She hesitated. "But she brought up some things I'd never thought of before."

"Like?" I wasn't opposed to hearing more. If there were a better way to do this—one where we could all be happy—then I'd jump at the opportunity.

"Like the fact that one day Eli will be mature enough to see that you and his mother are miserable," Rebel said. "And then he'll feel guilty for being the one thing that made you two stay together."

I sat up in bed, thinking about that. "He's happy right now, Rebel. You should see his face when we go down to eat breakfast. And that's because he's so happy his mother will be waiting at the table for him."

"If Tara would do what's right by him, then Eli would get to see her nearly as much. She's got to understand that you've found someone else. You're in love with someone, Harman. Someone who misses you and wants this to end." And there it was, Rebel wasn't going to go along with things anymore.

I'd never wanted to fight with her. I'd never wanted to hurt her. And it was hard arguing with her when we both wanted the same thing. But Eli had to come first. "Do you think I don't miss you, Rebel? I do. You're nearly all I think about. But I happen to think that Eli will respect his mother and me more, knowing that we put our own happiness to the side to make sure he was happy."

She cleared her throat before giving her reply, "Eli was happy when you and I were together, too."

He was; she was right about that. "But he wasn't entirely happy, Rebel."

"Only because Tara wasn't doing right by him. It wasn't anything you did—it was her. She had every opportunity to make him happy, Harman. And she never showed an ounce of respect for you, your feelings, or our relationship. She doesn't respect it at all."

Listening, Harmon knew Rebel was right about that. "I know." I didn't know what to do about it though. This was the only way I could get Tara to try, to get her into therapy and to start learning how to be a mother. "This is a complex situation."

"Tell me how your home life is going for you, Harman," she said. "Tell me if your home feels comfortable to you now that she's there."

It didn't. Certainly not to me, and not even to Eli at times. "I've had to put my foot down about a few things, but that's how things go with families. You don't understand because you've never been married and had a child with someone."

"I've wondered something this last week, Harman," she said. "If I were pregnant, then what would we do about this situation?"

For a second I thought she was trying to tell me she was pregnant. And for that split second, I felt joy rush through me. But then I remembered she was on the shot. "You're not, so that's a moot point."

"But let's just go with it for a moment. I'm pregnant. What are we going to do?" she asked.

My mind raced with what I would've done had that been the case. "I suppose we'd have no choice but to make things work. Tara would have to understand and let us do what we had to. Get married and raise our family together. But Tara would still have to be included— for Eli's sake."

"And if I said I could handle that?" she asked.

"You could. I know *you* could. That's never been the problem, baby." It wasn't Rebel who couldn't deal with that situation. "It's Tara. *She's* the one who has difficulty adjusting."

"And that's the excuse for this whole thing. Tara has a problem adjusting to the fact that you've fallen in love with someone else and your son has affection for someone else." She got quiet, then added, "It seems to me there are a number of people here being very selfless and who are willing to compromise, and one person who is not. Is that fair?"

"Life's not fair." I'd learned that long ago. "At this time, I only want to think about Eli. I want to see my son's smiling face each morning. And if that means that I have to live with my ex and be alone for the foreseeable future—then I'm sorry, Rebel. I'm going to do that. Even if it breaks my heart."

"And what do you think Tara will do when she realizes you'll never love her, Harman? How long will it be until that happens?" Her question stirred something inside of me.

I'd had my doubts about Tara's commitment to this thing as well. "I have no idea. But at least it will be her leaving, and not me telling her to go."

"And what effect do you think *that* will have on Eli?" she asked. "Letting him see her as the bad guy?"

"I don't think of it like that." I was trying very hard not to make Tara out to be the bad person in this thing. I didn't want my son thinking of his mother that way.

"I realize that my not agreeing with you might change your mind about me," she sounded a bit nervous. "But I can't sit by and not say anything. I don't think this is being handled the right way. And I've agonized over whether to talk to you about that or not. But I decided it wasn't like we were ever going to get back together, so why not tell you what I think?"

"How do you know we're not ever getting back together, Rebel?" As much as I'd been telling myself that I had to let Rebel move on, I just couldn't.

"If you stay with Tara in that loveless sham of a relationship, then you and I will never get back together, Harman," she let me know. I'd never heard her sound so certain, and it scared me. I couldn't let her go on believing that, even if it was best for her if she did.

"I'm not in a relationship with her, Rebel. We're merely living under the same roof, so we can raise our son together. We spend little to no time alone together." I thought about how the few small conversations we'd had almost always included a bit about Rebel. "Tara goes to her suite after dinner each night. We only see each other at breakfast and dinner."

"Sounds like something that could happen if you and I were together," she said. "If someone could make Tara see that keeping us apart isn't helping anyone. If only someone could talk to Tara and get her to understand that she has to take accountability for her own actions instead of trying to dictate how others can live their lives. If only someone could tell her that any relationship you have has absolutely no bearing on her relationship with her son, and that it's unacceptable for her to use Eli to try to keep you from the woman you love." Rebel had gotten so worked up at that point that she was practically panting. I couldn't tell if it was from frustration or from her trying to hold back tears. "But who'd do that?"

I felt like I'd been sucker punched.

Rebel was fighting for me—helping me to see things more clearly —and fighting for our relationship. And she was telling me it was time for me to fight for us, too.

Rebel's right.

28

REBEL

I DIDN'T FEEL any better after my conversation with Harman. His opinion hadn't seemed to waver one bit with anything I'd said. The next day, I worked only a few hours in the morning, then took off after lunch. I didn't feel quite right. I didn't know if it was because the conversation had gone nowhere or what the problem was, but I felt off.

Nancy had caught me before I took off, asking if I'd talked to Harman about things. I told her about our conversation and how nothing had changed. She told me to be patient with him, that one conversation probably wouldn't be enough to make him see things more clearly.

I thought she must be right, and I tried not to feel so hopeless. But I was dragging my ass anyway. All I wanted was for things to go back to how they'd been before Tara came around demanding her old life back.

Heading to the grocery store near my neighborhood, I thought I'd treat myself to something expensive for dinner. Filet mignon sounded good to me. As I perused the aisles, I saw a woman in the wine department, and the number of bottles already in her basket caught my attention.

I scanned the basket, then looked up at the woman herself—it was Tara. I couldn't stop myself, "So, you having a party, Tara?"

When she looked at me, the dark circles underneath her eyes told me things weren't going as well at the Hunter household as I'd imagined. "Oh! Hi, Rebel." Her hand hovered above a bottle of red wine, then she dropped it. "No, I'm just picking out some bottles to keep in the wine chiller I had delivered yesterday."

"Oh," I said as I looked back at her basket. "For a second there I thought you might have developed a drinking problem." I tried to make it sound like a lighthearted joke, but it came out much cattier.

Running her hand through her auburn hair, she tried to smile, but it looked off. Then her lips curved downward into a frown. "Is it terrible that I feel as if I'm missing out on something by moving back in with Harman and our son?"

"You had a pretty busy life before—if you've given that all up then I'd imagine you're feeling a little out of sorts." I didn't know why the woman felt I was an appropriate person to confide in. "But that sounds like something you should be speaking to your therapist about. You are still going to counseling, right?"

She smiled a little, looking down at the floor almost shyly. "Yes, I am. My therapist keeps telling me I need to work on setting and respecting proper boundaries—and yet here I am, spilling my guts to the very last person I should be."

I didn't know what to say to that. I definitely agreed with her therapist, but I found it a bit surprising that Tara did. If Tara had respected Harman's boundaries in the beginning, respected that he had started to carve out his own life for himself, well then, we might not have ended up in this mess.

"Your life has gone through a lot of changes lately. That would be difficult for anyone," I said, not unsympathetically.

"Yeah." She put back one of the bottles of wine. "And I've been using the wine to help me adjust to things. It's not helping. I thought getting rid of my home would make it easier to accept that I'd be going back to the life I left behind. But I find that I miss that independence—and it's not getting any easier." She shifted her weight, looking a bit like she wished she had just kept her mouth shut.

I sighed, not knowing what to say. On the one hand, I felt sorry for the woman and empathized with her confusion. But on the other, I couldn't ignore the fact that Tara's immaturity and insecurity was wreaking havoc on my own life.

"This is what you said you wanted, Tara," I kept my voice neutral, feeling too exhausted to muster any kind of emotion anyway. "If you're unsure about this, then you need to figure that out quick and say something. This kind of instability isn't good for a kid, and if you really want to do right by Eli, you need to make a choice and stick to it.

"The amount of time and effort you put in with your son does not have to be dependent on the man you're with—you can find a way to be there for him on your own, without Harman." I knew it was time to shut my mouth. I'd already butted in more than I should have, and I was probably the last person Tara would listen to. "You probably don't want to hear that right now, least of all from me. But I had to say something."

Her green eyes held steady on mine. "I don't hate you, you know."

Laughing a little, I said, "And I don't hate you, either. I just wish things could be different."

She looked at me, and I saw the fear in her eyes. "I don't want to lose my son to you."

"I would never let that happen, Tara." The fact that she still thought that told me there was still a lot she didn't understand. "I love Eli, Tara. But I'm not his mother, nor do I want to take your place. Even if Harman and I had never developed feelings for each other, I would still have cared about your son. But I do love Harman, and that means that he and Eli are a package deal. We can handle this, Tara. I can give you all the room you need to be that boy's mother. And when you're off happily living your life the way you want, with the people you want, you can rest assured that your son is in good hands."

"I have always been sure of that when he's with his father," she frowned down at the floor, as if she was struggling with this part of our conversation.

"You've dated, Tara. And when you did, Harman gave you the freedom to see whoever you wanted," I reminded her.

"But I never took anyone around my son." We still weren't quite on the same page.

"And that's your choice to make. If there weren't any men you were ready to introduce your son to, then you made the right choice in keeping them separate." But I hoped that wouldn't always be the case. "One day, you will find someone, Tara. Someone you'll want to share your entire life with—and that means introducing them to Eli. And that guy will need to become part of your son's life, too."

"Do you really think I'll find the right man for me, Rebel?" She looked at me as if she'd thought that an impossibility. "I haven't found him yet."

My heart skipped a beat at that. Did she finally realize that Harman wasn't the man for her? "One thing's for sure, you won't find him if you're living with an ex-husband you don't even love. And it's okay that you don't love him. In fact, I'd be lying if I didn't say that I'm so relieved to hear that. But don't hold onto Harman just because he's all you've ever known when it comes to your son."

"I think it would kill Harman if his son ever looked at another man as his father," she said quietly.

"That's just the thing, Tara. Eli won't ever see anyone else as his father—not while Harman is still in his life. Just as Eli won't ever see me as his mother, not so long as he has you. And I will never get in your way with him."

"But I don't know how to be there for him without physically being there." Her eyes were pleading now, as if begging me to give her the answers. "When Harman and I were separated, I didn't know how to integrate Eli into my new life."

"We can help you figure it out. You and Harman can learn to communicate better and learn how to be better co-parents." I didn't want her to think I was only saying this because I wanted to be with Harman. I did want to be with him, but I also wanted Eli to have two happy, attentive parents. "Even if I'm not in the picture, that's something you and Harman need to learn how to do."

Tara nodded her head, and I felt like she was finally listening to what I was saying. She was finally hearing what Harman and I had been trying to tell her all long.

"I think I have some thinking to do," she said as she started placing all of the wine bottles back on the shelf.

29

HARMAN

ALL DAY I'd thought about my call with Rebel from the night before. The more her words sank in, the more I thought she was on to something.

Eli and I sat in our favorite café after I'd picked him up from karate practice. He took a big bite of his burger as I sipped on a strawberry milkshake. Finally, I got up the nerve to ask him something I'd been wanting to speak to him about for a while. "So, about Rebel."

Gulping down the bite, he stopped me from saying another word. "Dad, I miss her. And I know you do, too. You're all frowny now. Even worse than you were before you met her. And I'm sad, too, Dad. I want her in my life."

"Me, too." But what would Tara think about that? "I'm just afraid your mother won't be on board with Rebel being around, Little Buddy."

"*Make* her get on board, Dad." He looked at me as if it was a no-brainer. And maybe he was right.

By the time we left, Eli was happy and optimistic that Rebel would be back in our lives shortly. He talked the whole way home about what kinds of things we could all do together—me, him, Tara, and Rebel. I didn't want to burst his bubble.

Just as I parked in our garage and got out of the car, I heard the sound of another car coming up the drive. When one of the other garage doors opened, I saw Tara's car pulling in.

Eli and I waited for her to get out and when she did, she had this look on her face that I'd never seen before. I'd seen her determined look, but this was like that but on steroids. She snapped her fingers as she passed us. "Harman, we need to talk. Eli, go up and take a shower. We'll be up later to tuck you in."

Eli and I looked at each other, neither of us sure what was going on, but we followed after her. He took off to take a shower, and I followed her to her suite where she pointed at the sofa. "Sit, please."

Taking a seat, I realized I'd never been in this position with her. "Tara, what's going on?"

She paced in front of me in silence for a moment. "This isn't healthy for any of us, Harman," she finally said. "And I liked—no, loved—my home. I just didn't know how to make things work with Eli, and I panicked when Rebel came into the picture. I'm sorry for what I've put you through, but I think I can make things work. I can come over here more. Like every morning. And even at dinner, too. Right? I can do that, and you can let me."

"Of course, you can do that." I'd never stopped her from coming to see her son and never would. I was too surprised by everything else Tara was saying to muster more of a reply.

But she wasn't done talking, anyway. She stopped pacing to look me in the eyes. "I don't love you, Harman. I was just confused, and I panicked—I was afraid I was going to be alone forever while you got to live some perfect happy life, and I fixated on my issues with Eli. After working on things with my therapist and speaking to...other people, I realize that now. I am so sorry, and I hope you will be able to forgive me.

"I do care about you and always will, plus we do have a son together. We will need to get along for him. But we don't have to live together, and we don't have to live our lives without love in them. And Rebel loves you. She really does. And I think she's a good person, too.

I believe her now when she says she'll never try to take my place with Eli."

"I do. too." I couldn't believe it. I wondered where this change of heart came from—if Tara had gone to Rebel despite me telling her off. I couldn't be mad at that, as it seemed Rebel had gotten through to her. For once in my life, Tara and I were on the same page. "And as I told you before, I don't love you either. But I do care about you and want you to be the mother to our son that you need to be. I won't stand in your way either, and I'll help you however I can."

"Rebel said that, too." She fisted her hands at her sides. "And Harman, I want you to treat me like an adult. I'm Eli's parent just as you are. I know you see me as that same dumb kid I was when we had to get married, but I'm grown now. Or I'm trying to grow. And it might take some time to get to the place you are, but I will get there."

That accusation caught me off guard, but I couldn't argue it. "I think you're right. And I think we still need therapy, Tara. You and I need to learn how to grow as Eli's parents. We've made a lot of mistakes, but I think we can do better going forward. We can help Eli cope with anything, and we don't have to be together to do that," I took a deep breath, finally believing those words. "So, what are we going to do next?"

"I'm taking my house off the market and moving back in to my place. But things are going to be different, okay?" She was so happy she was glowing. "I'm going to make up a bedroom for Eli there. I want him to feel as at home there as he feels here. But I'll still come over like I said—for most breakfasts and dinners. Only I'll have him every other weekend at my place. But I will see my son every single day that I possibly can."

"You don't know how happy that makes me. And it's going to make Eli *incredibly* happy." And that's all either of us had ever wanted.

"He can have all of us," she said with a smile and a twinkle in her eye.

"*We* can have it all," I agreed. "And I can't wait to tell Rebel the great news."

30
———

REBEL

CHRISTMAS MORNING, **one year later...**

"Santa came!" Eli shouted as he ran in front of us to the Christmas Tree Room. The first hint of Santa's visit was the now-empty plate of cookies Eli had left out for him on the kitchen table. He pointed at the empty plate. "He ate them all!"

I walked along behind the excited boy, Harman's arm wrapped loosely around my shoulders. Kissing the side of my head, he whispered, "I can't wait until he opens that Christmas card we gave him."

"Me, too." Harman and I had quite the surprise for Eli.

He threw open the door to the festive room and there stood Tara and Mark, her boyfriend. "Eli, there you are," Tara said as she held out her arms. Eli ran right into them, hugging her tight. "Merry Christmas."

"Merry Christmas, Mom." He let go of her to hug Mark. "Merry Christmas to you, too, Mark."

"And a Merry Christmas to you, my man," Mark said.

Tara had met Mark when he came over to install a Jacuzzi tub in the one of her bathrooms—per Eli's request. The two had hit it off right away, though Tara had needed some wooing as she'd decided to take a hiatus from men for a while. That lasted a whole month before

Mark's natural charm wore her down and the two became inseparable.

"Can I open presents now?" Eli asked his father.

"You can. Get to it, Little Buddy," Harman said. Watching his son, he took my hand in his and pulled it up to his lips, kissing the wedding band on my finger. He looked at me with glistening eyes. "Our first Christmas as a married couple. It feels different than last year, doesn't it?"

I nodded, wearing a goofy, ecstatically happy smile on my face. "So different. I can't believe it's been six months since we tied the knot."

Tara laughed. "Me neither. It seems like just yesterday we were in the backyard, celebrating that joyous occasion."

Eli took center stage as he opened the present from his mother. "Yes! A rocket launcher! Man, I've been needing this, Mom. Thanks." He ran to give her a hug and kiss then ran right back to the pile of presents. "This one is from Mark." He pulled the wrapping paper away to find a rocket to go with the launcher. "Oh, yeah!" He ran to Mark, hugging him. "Thanks, Mark. This is the best Christmas ever."

I hoped he'd keep thinking that after he found the Christmas card his dad and I had slipped into the pile of presents. "That's from Rebel and me, Eli," Harman pointed it out.

Looking a little confused, Eli opened the envelope and a gift card fell out. "Oops." He reached down to pick it up, tossing the card on the table nearby. "Thanks for the gift card, guys."

I looked at Harman with a little disappointment in my eyes. "Um, the card, Harman. He needs to read the card."

"I know." Harman pick the card up and handed it to Eli, who'd already moved on to the next present. "Here, Eli. Read what we wrote inside."

Rolling his eyes, he said, "Is it something sweet that's gonna make you guys cry? 'Cause I hate when I have to read something that makes you all cry."

Harman put the card in his son's hand. "Just read it."

Eli opened the card and read it out loud, "Merry Christmas, Big

Brother." He looked up at me then at my stomach. "Are you going to have a baby, Rebel? Am I going to be a big brother?" He always was a smart one.

I nodded, and the boy rushed at me, hugging me much tighter than usual. "Are you happy, Eli?"

"Yeah! I'm gonna be a big brother!" He couldn't fake all that joy I saw in his face when he finally let me go to hug his dad. "Thanks, Dad."

Tara came to me with teary eyes, hugging me. "Congratulations, Momma."

"Thank you." I cried right along with her. "I've never been happier."

"How far along are you, Rebel?" Mark asked.

"Two months." I knew I had a long way to go. "The morning sickness started a few days ago. That alerted me to the fact I was late, and we took the test. It's early still, but we thought this was the perfect occasion to spread the good news."

Mark nodded, then took Tara's hand. "I've been waiting for this day, too."

Eli, Harman, and I watched as Mark got down on one knee in front of Tara. When he pulled out a diamond ring from his pocket, I couldn't hold back the onslaught of tears. "Tara Marie Hunter, will you do me the great honor of becoming my wife?" he asked.

"Yes!" she squealed when he slid the ring on her finger, and I could see tears streaming down her face.

"Seems we all have good news this Christmas," Harman said with a smile on his handsome face.

Eli jumped up and down. "Yes! This is the most amazing Christmas ever!"

Later, after opening all our presents and eating the lavish meal Rene had prepared for us all to enjoy, I lay in bed watching Harman prowl toward me. His eyes moved over my sheet-covered body before slowly pulling it back.

Naked, I lay there on my back as he ran his hand over my stomach. "I can't believe this, Rebel. I'm getting to have a baby with the love of my life. Can it get any better than this?"

Laughing, I thought about everything we had to look forward to. "I hope you still feel that way when you've got to get up every two hours to help feed the baby. And when you get to change those nasty poopy diapers, I hope you still think it can't get any better than this."

"Oh, I know what I'm in for." He kissed my belly. "I'll love every minute of it."

When he looked back at me, he had fire in his eyes. Dropping his pajama bottoms, he moved fluidly, covering my body with his as I spread my legs to accept him.

As he pushed his hard cock into me, I moaned with desire. "What you do to me is beyond amazing, Harman Hunter."

His lips grazed my neck as he moved slowly. "I'm trying to go above and beyond with you, Rebel Hunter."

Pulling my foot up the back of his leg, I was happy he tried so hard for me. "You're quite the overachiever."

His warm breath against my ear made a shiver run through me. His teeth caught my earlobe, biting it, sending another chill through my body. Moving a little faster, he took me even higher, nibbling my neck and making me crazy with desire.

I raked my nails across his back as I arched up to meet his hard thrusts. What had started out slow and easy had become hard and savage. The sound of our hard breathing echoed off the walls of our large bedroom. Then the crescendo came as my body gave in, and his followed right along.

Panting, we lay perfectly still. Then his lips pressed against mine for a moment. When he pulled his mouth away, he gazed deeply, lovingly into my eyes. "*You* are my gift, Rebel. You always have been."

Running my hand through his wavy hair, I stared back, knowing without a doubt that our love was made to last a lifetime. "Harman Hunter, you're my gift, too. I never knew love until I found it in you. And now you've made me into a mother. I can't thank you enough for that."

"You already were a mother. Eli loves you like one, and you treat him the way a mother would." He kissed me again. "You're golden in my eyes, baby. Pure gold. And I'll cherish you until my last breath."

"I don't even want to think about that day, Harman." I closed my eyes and tried to get the thought of losing him one day out of my mind. "I never want this to end."

He kissed my lips again, taking my mind off of everything else. Moving inside of me again, he sparked up the flame that always simmered between us. It amazed me how easily that man could take my mind off of anything.

He took me around the moon one more time, then we lay there, panting again. The sound of my cell dinging with a text message had me turning my head to look at the nightstand. "I wonder who'd be texting me at this hour."

Harman smiled as he leaned up on his arm, resting his head on his palm. "Yeah, I wonder who it could be."

Picking up the phone, I saw it was from a number I didn't have stored in my contacts. "It's some random number." I put the phone back down. "Probably some sales thingy."

"Baby, read the message." He reached across me to pick up the phone.

He'd cooked something up, that was for sure. So I took the phone and opened the message. I had to blink a few times before I let myself believe it. "No way."

"Seems you got picked, Doctor Hunter." Harman smiled, then took the phone away from me, putting it back on the nightstand. "And before you go accusing me of favoritism, you need to remember that I took myself off the board that picked the winners. Your essay won fair and square."

I hadn't let Harman pay off any of my student loans. I felt like it wasn't fair if he paid them off for me. But I did enter the contest he'd funded—and apparently I'd won. "Out of five thousand plus entries, my essay was chosen?" I couldn't believe it.

Leaning in, he kissed me on the forehead. "They chose twenty winners. Seems you made that list. I'm proud of you, Doctor Hunter."

I had worked hard on that essay, and I felt a swelling of pride. "So

I guess if I ever get tired of being a veterinarian, I could become a writer. I must be better than I thought."

He nodded. "I did read your paper, Rebel. I read all the winning papers. And I'll be honest with—"

"Uh oh, not too honest, I hope," I interrupted him. I pushed him to lie back, then cuddled up against him.

He kissed the top of my head. "Out of the twenty papers I read, yours was the best by a longshot."

"You're just saying that because you love me." I kissed his chest then ran my hand up to rest on it.

"No, I'm not. There were no names on the papers. I picked that as the standout essay before the board gave me the names of the winners." He hugged me tightly. "I'd picked yours without knowing you wrote it. Crazy, huh?"

"It seems you and I just have something special. I'd pick you a hundred times over, Harman."

We'd all found our happily ever after, and I prayed it would go on for a very long time.

THE END

Did you like this book? Then you'll LOVE The Doctor's Nanny: A Single Dad & Nanny Romance (Saved by the Doctor Three)

She was there for me, but she wasn't supposed to make me feel the way she did...
When my wife died, it left a hole the size of Texas in my heart.
Alone with our young daughter, I needed assistance.
That's when I found her.
Or did she find me? Young, beautiful, and insightful beyond her years, she saved me from making a terrible mistake.
Did I make one anyway when I hired her and brought her into my home?

It didn't feel like a mistake when I took her into my arms and showed her what it's like to be a woman.

In my lifetime I'd learned when things are going great, something happens to make it disappear.

Would it happen to me again?

Start Reading The Doctor's Nanny

https://books2read.com/u/bowMMR

31

WHAT THE DOCTOR ORDERS EXTENDED EPILOGUE

TWO YEARS LATER...

Harman

"Catch him, Eli!" I shouted as we raced to stop fifteen-month-old Peyton before he got to the staircase. Someone had accidentally forgotten to babyproof it with the special gate that went there. "You know the renegade that boy is. He'll try to walk up those stairs, and he'll end up with a broken neck when he falls."

Peyton came into the world a bit harder than most, coming in breech and having to be taken by C-section at the last minute when he proved too stubborn to turn around—even with help from the doctor. He had a relentless spirit that had him doing everything months before other babies did. He walked at seven months, making our lives a lot harder before we were prepared for it.

Zipping past me, Rebel beat both of us to grab our son. "Gotchya." She scooped him up in her arms as he giggled and wiggled to get away. "Harman, can you find that gate and put it up before our little renegade kills himself?"

"On it," Eli said before I could say a thing. "I think the maid's still cleaning up there. That's why it's off."

It wasn't her fault. We weren't supposed to be back home yet. But we'd cut our vacation to Tahiti by half as long. When we got the call from Mark about his and Tara's twins coming early, we headed back to Seattle.

Tara's blood pressure was going through the roof, and her doctor wanted to take the twins earlier than initially planned. Eli wanted to be there when his new baby sisters were born. I felt it worth the early come back for our son to be there when his next two siblings arrived.

Rebel's cell rang in her pocket, and she fished it out as she wrangled our son who was trying desperately to get out of her grip, so he could make it up those stairs before his big brother returned with the gate to make that an impossibility. She looked at me after seeing who the call came from. "It's Tara."

"I hope everything's alright." I went to take Peyton from her, so she could answer the call without him distracting her.

"Hi, Tara," Rebel greeted her as Eli came back with the gate, securing the staircase. "Is everything okay?"

"Not really. A spike in my blood pressure has them moving things up even more," I could hear Tara say. "I'd really appreciate it if you guys could get Eli up here to see me before they take me into surgery. I'm not feeling right, Rebel. To tell the truth, it's scaring me."

Eli came to us after putting up the gate. "Is that, Mom?"

Rebel nodded. "Yeah. We're going to get you up there as fast as we can, Eli. The doctor's moved things up. She's going to have the twins today, not tomorrow the way she'd expected."

Eli held out his hand. "Can I talk to Mom?"

Rebel handed him the phone. "Sure, Slugger."

"Mom, are you okay?" he asked.

"Eli, I think I'll be fine. I just feel out of sorts," she told him. "And I've got this urge to see you before they take me into surgery."

"Okay, Mom," he said as he put on a brave face. "We'll be there soon."

Heading back to the garage, we all got back into the suburban then headed to the hospital. Rebel and I exchanged nervous glances, knowing Tara's situation was a dangerous one.

When we got up to the hospital and came into the maternity

ward, we knew things were about as bad as they could get. Nurses rushed around, half of them going into the same room we were headed to.

Eli's face went pale. "Something's wrong, Dad." He broke into a run, and we followed as best we could through the crowd.

When Code Blue came out over the intercom system, I knew Tara, and her twins were in dire straits. "Shit!"

Rebel had our son up in her arms and she, too, went pale. "Oh, God!"

Eli never made it into the room as the medical staff couldn't allow anyone else in the room as they tried to resuscitate Tara. He came to me, his expression frantic. "Dad, what's happening?"

"I'm not sure. We'll just have to wait here, Son." I put my arm around his shoulders as I tried to lend him some of my strength. I knew the boy was scared to death.

The sound of the one long beep stopped, then it started making the right sound, beeping intermittently. Rebel and I looked at each other with a little relief in our eyes. She whispered, "Good."

Nodding, I said, "They need to get the babies out, and things will get better."

I had hardly gotten the words out of my mouth when Tara was brought out, bed and all. They made their way to the OR, every person on her medical team wore worried expressions.

And Mark trailed behind, a nurse trying to console him, "I'm sure she'll be fine. Once the babies are out, we can do a lot more for your wife."

Mark's eyes found mine, and he came to me. "Why does it have to be this way?"

I had no answer for him. Shaking my head, I said, "We have to have faith that everything will be okay."

Rebel handed the baby to me, then held out her arms for Mark who moved right into them, and then he let out a sob that made my heart hurt for him. "Why?" he cried. "If I would've known this would happen to her, I wouldn't have ever asked her to have a baby."

"I know you wouldn't have," Rebel spoke quietly to him. "I know

I'm just a vet, but I've seen this happen in lots of animals. I can tell you that once they have the babies out, the process of getting Tara's blood pressure to stabilize will happen quickly."

Gulping back another sob, Mark moved out of Rebel's arms. "Okay. I believe you." He bent down and reached for Eli, hugging him. "She's going to be okay, Eli. And you'll never have to worry about her going through this again."

Rebel and I looked at each other with concern. It was evident that Mark would never want them to have any more children. And unless Tara was sterilized, then any future pregnancies would most likely be met with disapproval.

Rebel

Thirty minutes went by without a word from the OR. Mark and Eli sat next to each other in the waiting room as Harman and I tried to keep Peyton from running out of it and terrorizing the rest of the hospital.

When a nurse came out of the double doors, Harman and I both locked eyes on her. She wiggled her finger at Harman. "Doctor Hunter, can I talk to you?"

Now I was really anxious. I knew she would only be talking to him if things were horrible with Tara. Otherwise, she'd be talking to Mark. And when Harman turned to come back to me, the ashen color of his face let me know things had gone terribly wrong.

He took my hand, pulling me back with him to where Mark and Eli sat, looking worried as hell. Mark stood up. "What is it? I know it's bad. The only reason for that nurse to talk to you instead of me means that something's gone wrong."

Harman put his hand on Mark's shoulder. "Tara's had a stroke."

I put my hand on my chest, feeling like I might faint. Then I looked at Eli's shocked expression and grabbed him up, hugging him as he began to cry. "It's okay, Eli. She can recover." I looked at Harman through teary eyes. "Right?"

He nodded. "Mark's going to need help with the twins. Tara's going to be incapacitated for a while. But I'll make sure she gets the best rehabilitation."

"My babies are okay?" Mark asked.

Eli watched his father as he gave the news everyone wanted to hear, "They're okay."

Everyone breathed a sigh of relief, then I let Mark know he wasn't going to be alone. "You guys can come home with us, Mark. We'll all help you with the babies until Tara's better."

Eli's arms wrapped around Peyton and me. "Thank you, Rebel. You're the best ever."

Mark nodded. "I'll take that offer. I don't know what I would do if I were left alone to try to care for our babies." Tears ran down his cheeks as he turned his attention to Harman. "Is that okay with you, Harman?"

"I wouldn't have it any other way, Mark." Harman gave the man who'd married his ex-wife a hug. "You're not alone in this. You've got all of us."

When another nurse came out, she went straight to Mark. "Mr. Cofield, you can come back to see your daughters now."

"Okay." He wiped his eyes with the backs of his hands. Then he looked at me. "Can you come with me, Rebel? I don't feel very stable right now."

Handing Peyton to Harman, I said, "Of course, I'll come with you."

We followed the nurse to the nursery where the twins laid, sleeping quietly in their bassinets. Pink beanies adorned their tiny heads. "They both weigh three pounds and four ounces. They'll be with us until they reach five pounds. But you can be here as much as you want," the nurse pointed out.

Mark looked at me, then back at the nurse. "Can I let this woman and her husband come to see them, too?"

She looked at me. "You're Mrs. Cofield's son's step-mother, right?"

I nodded. "I am."

"Well, that makes you family. I don't see why you can't be on the list," she said. "And your husband, too. We'll have to get your identification. I'll take care of that before you guys leave today."

Mark sighed as he looked at his tiny babies. "They're here. I'm a father now. I didn't really feel it until now." He looked at me. "It's terrifying."

Nodding, I knew what he was talking about. "You'll get used to being afraid all the time. I know that sounds crazy, but it's true."

"I've got to take you back with me, Mr. Cofield. You've got papers to sign for your wife's rehabilitation." She led him away, and he looked back at me. "Can you come with me?"

Nodding, I followed them, coming up to walk beside him. I had no idea how he felt. He had two babies to take care of and a wife who might not be the same woman he'd fallen in love with, once she got better.

Mark might be taking care of all three of them before it was all said and done. I'm sure he felt that daunting. I knew I would've.

The nurse led us into the room they'd taken Tara to. She lay on the bed in an unconscious state. One side of her face drooped in a horrible fashion. And then I was glad that I'd come with Mark.

Falling to his knees beside his wife's bed, he lost himself in grief. I rested my hand on his shoulder to let him know I was there for him. The nurse and I exchanged looks that said we'd fix it all if we only could.

Unfortunately, only time would heal this kind of pain—a pain I prayed I would never have to feel. If I saw Harman like that, I didn't know what I would've done. Most likely, I would've fallen apart the same way Mark had.

With my free hand, I reached out to put it on Tara's forehead. "We're here for you, Tara. I promise you that we'll take good care of your husband and those beautiful baby girls of yours. You just rest and get better. I don't want you to worry about a thing. I'll be here for you as long as you need me to be."

Mark stood up, wiping his eyes, then hugged me. "Thank you, Rebel. You're an angel sent from above."

I didn't know about that, but I knew when it came to family, I would do anything to help.

~

Harman

Two months passed, and Mark was finally getting to bring his daughters home. We'd set up the suite of rooms Tara had stayed in before for Mark and the babies. Keeping the twins in the first room would allow us to help him out with them, letting him get some sleep as we all took shifts throughout the night.

Tara had suffered a massive stroke and still had trouble speaking. But I'd made sure she was getting the best help possible and she had made improvements. And she'd gotten to hold her babies for a short time that day when we'd stopped by the nursing home.

Sitting up in bed, her green eyes shone as Mark walked in, carrying their babies. "Hi, gorgeous," he greeted her. "Look who I have here."

Tara's lopsided smile made my heart ache. The paralysis hadn't let up much, and the left side of her face drooped. Her left arm and leg weren't working either. Her eyes moved back and forth rapidly as I knew words had come into her head but wouldn't make it out of her mouth.

Mark kissed her on the forehead. "I know, baby." He put one of the girls into Tara's right arm. "This is Betty." He ran his finger over the name he'd had printed on her onesie. "I've had their names put on most of their clothing, so we can know who's who. Having tiny identical twins isn't easy."

It was Rebel's idea to keep their names on their clothes until we had a chance to get to really know the girls. Her greatest fear was getting them mixed up and switching their identities.

Tara nodded, letting him know she agreed with what he'd done. She couldn't do any more than look at the baby she held but the way her eyes sparkled let us know how much she loved holding her new daughter.

Rebel leaned against my side, resting her head on my shoulder. "I think we should bring the babies to see her every single day, Harman. I think they'll help her progress more rapidly. I'm glad they finally gained enough weight to be let out of the hospital. I foresee Tara's progress moving a whole lot faster now that she can see and hold the girls."

I agreed. "Me, too."

Mark took Betty out of Tara's arms and replaced her with the other girl. "And this is Carol."

Tara looked at the baby for a long time before Mark took her back. When he did, Tara reached out with her right hand, touching him on the nose.

Mark looked confused until Rebel said, "She's telling you that Carol has your nose, Mark."

Tara nodded and gave Rebel a lopsided smile. Rebel moved in to give Tara a hug. "You've got very beautiful daughters, Tara. I'm envious of you." She looked back at me. "It's made me want to try for a girl. After we get through with helping you with yours, of course. I don't want you to worry about a thing. We've got your old rooms fixed up for your husband and babies. No one will go without being taken care of, Tara."

Tara patted Rebel's arm as she looked into her eyes. One tear ran down her cheek, then Rebel quickly wiped it away. Mark looked back at me, trying not to cry himself. I nodded, letting him know I wasn't having an easy time of it myself.

When Rebel walked away from Tara, I saw Tara pointing at me. Then she kissed her palm and held it out to me. I nodded. "You're very welcome. Your family is in good hands, Tara. All I want you to worry about is getting better for them."

Nodding, she closed her eyes, and we all watched as she fell asleep quickly. I knew she wanted to rest and let time heal her as fast as it could. Being unable to do anything for herself and her family had to have hit her hard. She'd been so happy about having the twins. Having another chance at having babies, and this time around she wasn't mad about having them, had made things much better for her.

As we left her room, Rebel took one of the babies from Mark. "Let me carry her out." She rubbed her nose against Carol's. "Your momma noticed you've got your daddy's nose, Carol. And now we've got a way to tell you and your sister apart since she's got your momma's nose."

Tara hadn't had any natural instincts with Eli. I was glad to see she'd formed some over the years. Even in her present state, she was already being more of a mother than she'd been to Eli when he was born.

As we headed out to the cars, I thought how sad it was that Tara had spent Eli's younger years oblivious of what a mother's role in her kid's life was. And now she was incapable of caring for her new babies. She would miss out on so much once again.

When we got to the cars in the parking lot of the nursing home, a bright idea struck me. "Hey, why don't we get full-time nurses for Tara? We could bring her home then. That way she'd get a lot more time with her babies." If I could do nothing else, I could give Tara more time with her children.

Mark looked at me with wide eyes. "Harman, you'd do that for us?"

Rebel patted me on the back. "Giving Tara as much time as she wants with her kids is one of Harman's great passions. And one of the things that makes me more than proud of him. I think that's a great idea. We can have the specialists come in, too. No need for Tara to have to be taken to therapy sessions. What good is money if you don't use it to help people, right?"

I nodded. "Right."

Rebel

Having Tara home too made things feel much better. Mark was happy, Eli was happy, the babies were happy, and Tara was over the moon. In only two weeks, she'd gotten her mouth to cooperate with her and now could talk with just a slight slur.

Her left arm and leg were up by ten percent, which might not sound like much, but to her, it meant she could actually move the limbs she'd been unable to.

I walked into the nursery to check on the sleeping twins and saw Tara sitting in one of the two rocking chairs in the room. She gazed at her sleeping babies, not even noticing me. For a moment, I stood still, thinking I might leave her to her thoughts. Then her eyes came to mine. "Hi."

"Hi," I said, not sure if I should stay or not. "Do you want time alone with your babies, Tara? I can leave."

Shaking her head, she looked at the chair next to her. "Come sit with me."

"I was just checking on them." I took the seat she'd offered. "I've fallen in love with your babies, Tara."

"All of them," she said with a much less droopy smile. "First Eli, and now Betty and Carol." Reaching over to touch the back of my hand, she asked, "How would you like to be their Godmother, Rebel? Mark and I were talking last night, and we know of no other people in this entire world who would make better Godparents to our daughters than you and Harman."

I couldn't believe it. She was sharing her children with us in a way I'd never imagined. "We would be honored, Tara. Truly honored."

A tear fell from her eye. "*I'm* honored, Rebel. I'm honored to have met you. You came into this family and made it into a real family. It's as if we were never broken. And now you'll make my daughters feel the same way you made my son feel—like part of you. Let me tell you that knowing you've got my back made this hard time a lot more tolerable."

"Good." I took her hand, holding it. "I never saw this coming, Tara. Not in a million years did I imagine a thing like this being my life. And I wouldn't change one single thing about it."

"I'm glad," she said. "Me, neither."

I thought I'd let her in on a secret Harman and I had. "Well, I'm trying to change one thing. Harman and I are trying for a little girl of our very own."

Tara smiled. "Good. Betty and Carol will have someone to play with. Peyton's a bit too rowdy for them, I'm afraid."

"Don't I know it." That boy was a little terror. I saw Peyton as a loner type who would probably get into as much trouble as he could find. "Maybe having a little sister will chill that boy out."

Tara laughed. "I wouldn't count on it. I saw him running past here this morning. He had a fireplace poker in his hand, laughing hysterically as he ran from Harman. It wasn't safe at all, but I couldn't help but laugh as that little boy with those short legs outran long-legged Harman."

"He's a freak of nature, that kid." I would've loved to blame Harman for Peyton's antics. But the truth was, I was a lot like that boy when I was a baby. Or so my parents said anyway. I had trouble believing them about that. They kept telling me Peyton would make a complete turnaround once he hit puberty, the way I had. All I could do was hope that was the case with my son.

"So, I'll wish for you to have a girl this time," Tara said. "And a calm little princess of one at that."

One of the babies stirred and I got up to see which one of them was waking up. Betty's green eyes opened, and I smiled at her. "Morning, Sweetheart." Picking her up, I kissed her on the forehead before handing her to Tara. "I'll go make her a bottle."

"Thank you," Tara said as she gazed at her daughter.

Going to the attached kitchenette, I made two bottles, knowing Betty's sister would soon wake up hungry as well. Mark came in, leaning on the doorframe. "Did Tara ask you and Harman about becoming godparents for our girls?"

"She did." I turned to him with a smile on my face. "And I've answered for my husband and me with a yes. It's an honor I didn't see coming."

"You both are heroes to my family and me," he said, making me blush. "I don't know what I would've done without you two."

I recalled a time when Tara had told me much the same thing

about Eli. She'd said Harman was his hero and when I entered the picture Eli looked at me as one, too. But I'd never thought that way. "I think anyone would've done the same thing Harman and I did, with money not being a problem."

"I think you're wrong." Mark crossed his arms over his chest. "My own parents told me there was nothing they could do. They've got their little plumbing business in Ohio that they couldn't take time away from. So, you're wrong. Most people don't take the time to care enough to offer their home and time to help others. You and Harman are a couple of unique individuals. To be honest, I thought your whole situation to be odd when I first came around. But now I see it for what it is. You guys are a true family where sharing blood doesn't matter. And you've pulled us into your family. It makes me feel special in a way I've never felt before."

"All this praise is making me embarrassed, Mark." I waved my hand at him. "Now, shoo. I've gotta get these bottles to your babies."

He took the bottles out of my hands. "No. I'll take care of them this time. Tara and I can handle it. You go find Harman and spend some time alone together. We've got Eli and Peyton for the night, too. Take a break. Let me take the weight for now. I can handle it."

"I know you can." I couldn't make the smile leave my face as I left their suite to go find my husband and take a break with him.

Harman

Sitting in the sunroom, I heard the door open. "There you are. Come on. We're getting the night off. Mark is handling things with everyone, including Eli and Peyton." Rebel came to me, taking me by the hands. "I'm thinking a hotel, jacuzzi tub, copious amounts of Jack and Coke, and you."

It had been months of hard work, but it was all worth it. "I'm with you."

Rebel led me upstairs to pack, letting me in on some news, "So, we've been asked to be Carol and Betty's godparents. I've accepted for us."

"I would've done the same." I pulled her into my arms, kicked our bedroom door closed, then kissed her with a desire I'd had to tamper down with the arrival of Tara's family.

We'd decided to try for a girl, but we'd had little to no time to do much trying. I thought we could get in a bit of baby making before we left to do more of the same.

Rebel's legs wrapped around me as I picked her up. She held on tightly while kissing me back with a hunger I could taste. We'd put so many people ahead of us for such a long time, taking time for us felt amazing.

Walking with her to the bed, I climbed up on it on my knees then laid her back, never letting our lips part. I wanted to keep contact with our bodies. I'd craved her for so long, and finally allowed to have her, I wanted all of her—and I wanted it now.

Pushing my hand under her shirt, I pushed her bra up, feeling her firm tit, the nipple growing harder and harder as I ground my swelling cock against her heating cunt.

Arching up to me, Rebel made a low growl as she ran her hands underneath my shirt, clawing my back. I sat up, pulling her shirt off over her head, then pulling mine off, too. Unhooking her bra, I took that off, too, and buried my face in her big tits.

"Harman," she panted. "Oh, baby, that feels so good."

Giving one a hard suck, I played with the other until she groaned. "You're about to make me come."

So I sucked harder until she was whimpering with an orgasm. Only then did I stop to pull her jeans off, then ripped her panties away from her dripping cunt.

Dropping my jeans, I got rid of everything else I had on, then moved my body over hers, thrusting my hard cock into her hot recesses. "Oh, yeah." She felt like home to me when I was inside of her. "Oh, baby. How do you do it? You're as tight as the first time."

Her nails raked across my shoulders. "Kegels." She did one, and I nearly shot my load into her with the insane feeling it gave me.

"Shit!" I grabbed her by the shoulders then flipped us around, so she was sitting on top of me. "Do that over and over, Baby."

She didn't ride me the way she usually did. This time she sat perfectly still, flexing her vagina to clench around my cock in short bursts that took me to a whole other world. "You like that?" she whispered hoarsely.

"It's almost like when you give me head, only way different." I couldn't describe it to her at that moment because my mind was mostly on that insane feeling going on around my cock. "Keep doing it. I can't get enough."

Placing her hands on my chest, she clenched her hot walls around me until I was about to blow. Then I turned her over quickly, making hard thrusts as I put one hand behind her right knee, pulling her leg up until her foot was above her shoulder.

She held my arms as she gasped for air. "You're about to make me come!"

Looking into her eyes, I asked one question, "You want to have my baby, Rebel Hunter?"

"God, yes!" she cried out as I felt her body contracting around my engorged cock.

I let it all go then, spilling my seed inside of her. Pushing my cock into her as deep as it could go, I tried my hardest to give her what she wanted. To see her belly swollen with my baby was what I wanted to see in the near future.

I stayed that way on top of her, letting my seed sit for a while, hopefully taking my little swimmers to where one would burrow its way into her egg that would become a living, breathing human being.

"The whole process amazes me," I groaned as a bit more sperm came out of me.

"Birth?" she asked as she'd finally gotten her breath back.

"Yeah, that and life itself." I kissed her lips softly. "I hope we have as little trouble getting pregnant as we did with Peyton."

"Me, too." She held up one hand, showing me crossed fingers. "And I hope we have a girl this time."

"Me, too." I kissed her again. "I love you. And I love our family."

"Me, too." She smiled up at me. "All of them."

If anyone would've told me that one day I'd have my ex-wife and her whole family living under the same roof with me and my new wife and kids, I would've said they were nuts. Certifiable.

But that's what had happened. And nine months from that very day, my wife and I had our baby girl to add to that crazy family. Little Olivia graced us and kept our happily ever after going stronger than ever.

The End

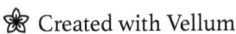 Created with Vellum

Ingram Content Group UK Ltd.
Milton Keynes UK
UKHW022122060323
418148UK00005B/268